The Mad Dog

Also by Heinrich Böll

The Silent Angel

The Train Was on Time

And Where Were You, Adam?

And Never Said a Word

The Bread of Those Early Years

Irish Journal

Tomorrow and Yesterday

Billiards at Half-Past Nine

The Clown

Absent Without Leave: Two Novellas

End of a Mission

Children Are Civilians Too

Group Portrait with Lady

The Lost Honor of Katharina Blum

Missing Persons and Other Essays

What's to Become of the Boy? or, Something to Do with Books

The Safety Net

Women in a River Landscape: A Novel in Dialogues and Soliloquies

A Soldier's Legacy

The Casualty

The Mad Dog

stories

Heinrich Böll

Translated by Breon Mitchell

St. Martin's Press New York

Originally published as *Der blasse Hund* by Verlag Kiepenheuer & Witsch in Cologne, Germany.

Design by Songhee Kim

Library of Congress Cataloging-in-Publication Data

Böll, Heinrich 1917–1985
[Short stories. English. Selections]
The mad dog : stories / Heinrich Böll ; translated by Breon Mitchell.
p. cm.
ISBN 0-312-16757-1
1. Böll, Heinrich, 1917– —Translations into English.
I. Mitchell, Breon. II. Title.
PT2603.0394M573 1997
833'.914—dc21 97-16104
CIP

First Edition: September 1997

10 9 8 7 6 5 4 3 2 1

contents

introduction

EARLY TREASURES CONTINUE TO EMERGE from the literary estate of Heinrich Böll. The sensation created in Germany in 1992 by the publication of the novel *Der Engel schwieg* (*The Silent Angel,* 1994) was due only in part to the obvious interest literary scholars took in the rediscovery of his first sustained work of fiction. More striking was the quality of the work itself. Although no German publisher would take a chance on it in 1950, fearing its vivid portrayal of the harsh realities of the war and its aftermath, the novel found immediate readers in the 1990s. It was not simply that Böll was now a literary icon. The novel spoke directly to the hearts of Germans, with a voice that remained clear, strong, and moving in spite of the intervening decades.

The response to *The Silent Angel* in America quickly reaffirmed that Böll's keen observation and poetic power remained an international affair. The universal themes of human loss and human courage, of spiritual despair and spiritual strength, rang clearly through the pages of the novel. American critics found *The Silent Angel* "a beautiful, urgent novel . . . as perfect as anything Böll ever wrote," "a haunting evocation of postwar desolation," and "still pertinent to our own hunger for the bread of meaning amid the rubble of history." The novel was recognized as a key to Böll's entire later development and praised as a magnificent work of art in its own right.

The present collection of hitherto unpublished short stories is of equal importance to readers everywhere. Like *The Silent Angel,* these tales may well have seemed too bleak for German publishers in the immediate aftermath of the war, but they offer powerful and striking insights into the human condition which still touch us today. They range in tone and subject matter from the prewar idealism of "Youth on Fire" to the grim despair of "The Mad Dog," and from scenes of battle to the daily lives of those who struggle to make sense of things when war has ended. Readers will hear echoes of almost every familiar motif from Böll's later work, but, paradoxically, they will be listening to the original source of those very themes.

Perhaps the most surprising story in the collection is "Die Brennenden" ("Youth on Fire"). There is good reason for our surprise: Böll wrote the story when he was nineteen years old, before he had completed the German equivalent of high school. It is thus the earliest of his stories to which we have ever had access, offering a unique, prewar perspective on the young writer. Its striking chords of youthful idealism, the search for spiritual meaning, and the role of the Catholic church already seem familiar, as do a keen eye for telling detail, a deep sympathy for the poor, and an impatience with social conventions and mores. There are also unusual reversals of plot: a young prostitute reveals herself to be a Christian in disguise, a concert pianist takes on a strange lover, a priest performs an unexpected marriage. From the opening scene of contemplated suicide to the closing vision of hope, the story reveals touches of the major writer to come.

"Youth on Fire," written in 1937, reminds us that Heinrich Böll was called to the writer's life from an early age. Although it is difficult to imagine what his stories and novels might have been like without the crucial, formative experience of World War Two, it is clear that the war did not create Böll's literary impetus, but only formed and channeled it. In the ten years that intervened between "Youth on Fire" and the earliest of the remaining stories in this collection, Böll's writing was limited almost exclusively to long and detailed letters to his wife.

The spiritual and creative distance covered as Böll absorbed the devastating impact of battle and defeat may be seen in "The Mad Dog," written in 1947, a story that reads like a hopeless cry of pain. Here a young man who might well have been one of the enthusiastic youths listening to Beethoven at the end of "Youth on Fire" is twisted and torn by his country and its fate, impelled toward murderous revenge in a world gone mad. Yet the connecting humanitarian thread remains, unbroken over the years.

The war leaves its imprint on every one of the remaining stories in the volume, from battle scenes to postwar poverty, from senseless destruction to the ruins of love. "The Tale of Berkovo Bridge," printed here for the first time in its original form, offers a powerful metaphor of the conflict of duty and compassion in time of war; "The Fugitive" and "Trapped in Paris" are breathless depictions of soldiers on the run, desperately seeking to avoid the face of death. Several of the stories show men and women searching for remnants of love amid spiritual wreckage, with varying degrees of success. A profound human sympathy permeates this book, a belief that God will forgive us, as we may perhaps one day forgive ourselves.

This collection closes with one of the most moving texts Böll ever wrote: "Paradise Lost." So strong was the hold of the images in this unfinished novel that Böll continued to rework passages from it into both novels and short stories over the next several years. Now at last we have the paradox of the original fragment rendered whole—for the ruined symmetrical garden through which the narrator passes, the mirrored images of memory and present moment, the arrival and departure which frame the tale, create a text of unexpected balance and harmony, a complex aesthetic whole as finished as any reader could desire, a classic story lost but now regained.

—Breon Mitchell

The Fugitive

HIS HEART POUNDING, HE WATCHED from his hiding place as the car raced along the country road, its headlights blazing. He jerked back as if struck in the face as the car squealed to a halt, then turned sharply and sent the merciless beam of its searchlight gliding slowly and deliberately back and forth across the fields. Trees flared in unnatural brightness, as if awakened to terrifying life by some magic spell. Bushes were drenched by the harsh, maniacal light before slipping back into darkness; then the beam was stopped short by the wall that hid him. He could almost feel the light damming up against it. Then it flowed across the crumbling top; he shut his eyes, blinded, struck by savage pain as the corrosive beam stabbed at his eyes through a crevice in the wall.

He heard the steady idling of the motor and men's voices; he listened intently as the searchlight was extinguished and the heavy weight of darkness fell over him again. Rising from the cold, damp meadow, he risked raising his head above the wall. The car was standing on the road with its searchlight stowed. He saw the silhouettes of two men, their faces seemingly turned toward him; surely they must sense that he was there . . . surely. His eyes bored deeply into the flat darkness, as if forcing it to reveal their faces. He had to know if Germat was there. Germat! His heart skipped a beat. If so, he was lost. Germat was the most cunning bloodhound in the entire zone, a vicious man-eater gifted with nearly supernatural instincts. The men's voices appeared almost apathetic, a steady murmur.

All at once he heard noises to the left and right in the dark field, like someone creeping, dragging his feet, and the unbearable yet unavoidable sucking sound of a boot being pulled from mud that has closed around it. My God . . . he had just realized his head must be visible above the wall, like a black oval against the darkened blue of the heavens, even at this distance. He ducked down, panting in brutish fear, and in the next split second, as he tried to bring the dizzying whirl of his thoughts and emotions under control, a bullet whizzed over the wall from the direction of the road, the signal that the hunt was officially on. Had he missed the gunshot in his first moment of panic?

Suddenly he felt totally weightless, strangely light, as if the ice-cold hatred in his heart had crystallized the chaos of fear and peril. He thought quickly yet carefully; now the veil lifted and he saw through their tactics: They had already outflanked him. He heard the sounds of several men to either side, and behind him as well. They probably had a chain of sentries all the way to the road, where Germat waited, directing the hunt with his devilish intellect. It was hopeless. He would be shot a dozen times if he made the slightest move in the darkness. They knew where he was, while he had no idea where they had stationed themselves; he could only head straight into the heart of the trap. Then suddenly he thought of a plan, laughably simple, dazzlingly bold. Hate gave him courage, a savage living hatred that served as well as love. He no longer felt cold, or hungry, or afraid. A deadly enemy stood before him; he had to attack with the strength of an ox and the boldness of genius. He heard the circle close behind him, heard two of the beaters meet behind the orchard wall and establish contact with a few soft words. Then he prayed, a short quick prayer, like a flame flaring up and extinguishing, and he almost felt like smiling, yes, smiling in the darkness, surrounded by hunters, yet almost sure of victory. He raised his hands high above the wall and cried out: "Don't shoot, Germat, I give up!" He heard the startled cries of the men around him, sprang quickly over the wall, and ran toward the road, smiling as he yelled: "Call off your dogs!"

The road was scarcely more than a hundred yards away and he ran quickly, before the troops could recover from their surprise, until he made out the tall figure of Germat through the darkness, standing in his black uniform, blacker than the blue of night. Still holding his hands over his head, he leaped across the ditch. Then, in the glow of the headlights, he had a clear view of Germat's hard, coldly handsome face, his mouth opening to speak with a satisfied smile. Gathering his whole body—his only weapon—he threw himself savagely against Germat with all the crazed fury of his hatred. He felt the impact with a thrill of pleasure, raced around the car, and heard the driver jump out with a yell, just as he had planned; then he lowered himself softly and carefully to the ground and crept slowly, silently, under the car. The low-lying gas tank left just enough space for him to see Germat: He lay two steps away from him on the cold, hard asphalt of the road. It took every ounce of will to suppress the deep, terrible sobbing rising within him. His entire body trembled. He broke out in a nervous sweat as the smell of gas and oil made his empty stomach lurch with nausea.

Almost as a diversion, to break the terrible tension, he looked toward Germat. He lay groaning and cursing on the road, his face twisted in bestial anger. Blood flowed onto the gray, cold, dully gleaming asphalt from a wound on the back of his head. The driver fumbled over him helplessly, managed to lift his head and place a seat cushion beneath it, as the cries of the troops rang out from the darkness.

Germat was now standing. Strickmann had bandaged him and handed him a few pills, which he washed down with brandy; he was leaning against the car. His boots, those elegant soft boots, which poor Gunderland had to polish each morning, stood directly before Joseph's eyes. For an instant he was seized by an insane desire to grab them and jerk backwards, toppling Germat flat on his face again. Yes, he might have risked his life to send that devil flying a second time, but what he heard now occupied his entire attention. Germat cut off the curses and empty threats of the guards in a cold voice and said irritably: "You should have stopped yapping and got right after the bastard . . . then we'd have him by now. All right, shine a light over here, Jupp . . ."; evidently he'd taken out a map. The men's feet gathered around his beautiful boots. "We're here—at the Breckdorf exit, there's the border; if he wants to cross it, he has to go back down the road we're on now. Damn, my head hurts! If we ever get hold of that swine . . . We've got to catch him, I tell you . . . that filthy dog." He groaned, stamped his feet, and continued: "All right, Berg and Strickmann, patrol the stretch from here to Eiershagen . . . right here, look. . . . Grosskamp and Strichninski, you cover the stretch between Brickheim and Gordelen. I'll drive back to camp and send reinforcements. Set them up so the entire sector is closed all the way to the border. Okay, you know what to do. . . . Damn it, pay some attention to the map." He seemed to be holding his head again, groaning and cursing. "Get going," he said. "I'll wait till you've taken your positions. Büttler, get the car turned around. . . ."

Joseph didn't realize the danger he was in until the engine suddenly revved up and the entire car began to vibrate. He broke out in a cold sweat, a deathly fear. His heart skipped a beat, and with the final ounce of strength in his weakened hands he clutched the rods beneath the car, then lifted his feet and wedged them somewhere between a metal pipe and the car's undercarriage, barely holding on. The car went into reverse to turn around, backed up to the ditch, the tires spun, and his grip slipped as the car lurched. Head down, his legs clamped fast, he dangled helplessly under the car as the tires continued to spin; he held back a scream welling up within him. Almost fainting from weakness, agitation, and terror, he grabbed on tight again, but could no longer suppress the tears. They streamed heavy and hot down his cheeks; he was blinded by the flood. . . .

Somewhere in his subconscious he registered the tilt of the car as Germat jumped onto the running board, but the tears kept flowing, as if the infinite pain of his lost state had broken through the shell of his will and was now pouring into the silence of the night.

He couldn't remember releasing his hands and feet. He felt the wheels race past his head like a final breath of horrible danger; then he found himself battered, dirty, tired and hungry, wet with tears, on the hard, bare road.

In that terrible solitude he almost wished himself back in the company of the hangman's lackeys, caught up in the insane tension of the chase.

The darkness had thickened; a mantle of night lay silent and heavy over the earth. To muffle his footsteps, Joseph left the road, treading on the soft soil of the fields, following the roadway toward Breckdorf. If he could only sit somewhere for just an hour or so, in a house with other people, eat something, clean up, warm himself; my God, just to see a few people other than those he'd been with behind barbed-wire for months, in the hangman's clutches. Just one hour, then he could slip past the sentries before reinforcements arrived and reach the border before dawn, and then . . . then perhaps freedom. . . .

Holding to the road, his senses tuned to the night, he reached the village, but it must have been late, for there wasn't a light anywhere. The black blocks of the houses rose dimly against the sky, the outline of the trees. He passed a farmyard sunk deep in silence, so close to the hedge that he brushed against the thorns. Then with startling suddenness the huge, uncanny silhouette of a church rose before him, a marvelously peaceful square, surrounded by tall trees, and a house in which a light still burned. He approached it slowly and cautiously; just don't start the dogs barking. . . . Germat's men would be on him like wolves.

His head ached terribly, a piercing pain, like a merciless finger probing his tormented brain. His face was scratched, he was filthy, soaked to the skin, and tired, so tired it took an effort to lift his foot at every step. Finally he was leaning against the dark door, feeling for the bell. It sounded bright and shrill within the hall, startling him. He heard a soft, rapid tread, the light clicked on and seeped under the door. My God, what if he'd dropped in on a hero of the Party by accident? But terror no longer held sway over his exhausted mind, and a sudden wave of nausea seemed to turn his stomach inside out. Dear God, just some rest, rest and a little bread . . .

He tumbled through the open door and gathered enough strength to whisper to the dark figure: "Quick . . . quick . . . shut the door. . . ."

Blinded by the light, overwhelmed by misery, he stood sobbing, pitiful and dirty, leaning against the wall, squinting painfully at the startled chaplain. Music, a fragment of some fading, melancholy melody, reached his ears, and it seemed as if the whole of mankind's dark longing for paradise were concentrated in that one brief phrase of music, sweet and heavy, clouded with sorrow. It struck him like a death blow; he fell as if shot.

When he opened his eyes again, he first saw only books. He stared at an entire wall of them, their bright titles gleaming softly in the dull glow of a desk lamp. He felt the warmth of a stove at his back; he was sitting in a large, soft armchair, with comfortable cushions, to his right a large, flat desk of dark-stained wood. A friendly man's voice asked: "Well?" and as he turned around with a start, he was looking into the narrow, pale face of the chaplain, bending over him. The first thing he noticed was the marvelous fragrance of good tobacco and good soap, mingled with the pleasant neutral odor of the confession box. Large, intelligent gray eyes peered at him from the white planes of the face, veiled by a cool reserve, regarding him with almost impersonal curiosity. Then came the second question: "What now?"

But Joseph was staring at the carpet, lost in dreams, a magnificent, clean, warm, yellow carpet, beautiful, tasteful etchings on the wall. A dream of domesticity and warmth, beauty and security, enveloped the room. The contrast with the sties they lived in at camp was so shocking that tears came to his eyes again. My God, this armchair, soft and human, actually made to sit on! The chaplain's pale face glanced nervously toward the desk, where a few books lay open and various papers were strewn about. "Well?" he asked again, but banished the impatient look from his face at once, as if he were ashamed. Joseph turned slowly to face him.

"Do you have something I could eat? I should wash up, too, and then . . . and then . . ." He stood up quickly and gestured helplessly at himself. "They're after me. . . . I have to be gone in half an hour. . . . My God, I'm dreaming. . . ." He tightened his hands impatiently into fists and stood trembling.

The chaplain spread his hands at once and said regretfully: "My housekeeper's—" but then interrupted himself, motioned for the pitiful figure to follow him, and stepped out into the hall. Joseph slipped after him.

"You're from the camp?" he asked on the way to the kitchen. Joseph mumbled hoarsely: "Yes." The kitchen was so sparkling clean it looked as if no one had ever cooked there. It seemed meant only for show; everything gleamed in the glow of the glass lamp, not a speck of dust to be seen, not a dish in sight. The cupboards were closed, and the stove was obviously ice cold. The chaplain tugged awkwardly at a cupboard. "For heaven's sake," he said, shaking his head, "she always takes the key with her. . . ." But Joseph had grabbed the poker from the tidy coal box and said tersely, with a strange, almost coldly cynical set to his lips: "If you'll permit me . . ." The chaplain turned, startled and concerned, but Joseph pushed him aside, wedged the poker between the doors of the cupboard, and forced it open with a jerk. He regarded the splendors with almost predatory eyes, sighing.

Indignation mixed with a slight disdain showed on the chaplain's face. He watched, clutching his hands nervously behind his back, as the man wolfed down thick slices of bread covered with butter and sausage. The ragged, filthy figure in greasy denim was a bizarre sight, with tousled, dirty hair and ravenous hunger in his large, gray, oddly gleaming eyes. The only sound in the stillness was his noisy chewing and at times a strange snuffling, as if the man had a cold and no handkerchief. The chaplain couldn't take his eyes off him, but the visitor no longer seemed to notice him.

It seemed as if time had stopped, and that the world consisted only of this kitchen in which he sat trembling beside a vagabond who ate and ate.

Joseph held the loaf of bread in his left hand and the knife in his right, seeming to hesitate; but then he dropped the knife on the table, shoved the bread aside, and stood up. "You could at least have offered me something to drink; you've never eaten a dozen slices like that," he said in genuine irritation, then went over to the sink, fished the soap from a niche in the wall with annoying self-confidence, and began washing his face, puffing noisily. He found the hand towels under a clean cloth behind the oven, as if he knew the layout of the house forward and backward. "Clean underwear, now that would be just fine . . . and my feet washed . . ." he mumbled through the hand towel, drying his face and head roughly, almost relishing it. He hung up the towel and was about to ask for a comb when he looked the chaplain full in the face for the first time. "My God," he said softly, with childlike amazement. "You're not angry with me, are you?"

"No," laughed the chaplain with an annoyed snort. "You're the most charming fellow I've ever met!" He stood waiting by the door. Shaking his head, Joseph walked past him into the hall, heading for the study. He was still shaking his head as he sat down again in the armchair.

The chaplain had turned off the outside lights, relocked the doors, and returned quickly, as if he were afraid to leave the man alone. His face was masked with a strange severity like that of a welfare worker.

"I'll need to ask you for a couple of other things," Joseph said, speaking in an almost businesslike tone. "First a comb; you know how it is, a person feels so unfinished somehow, when he's washed up but hasn't combed his hair . . . thanks." He took the black comb and combed his hair contentedly. "And a cigar, if you have one . . . and, I'm sorry, a sip of wine . . . then I think I'll make it across the border easily. I'm feeling stronger now and I'm not afraid anymore." The chaplain wordlessly handed him a cigar, along with a box of matches. "Now I know why the hangman's men, even though they're stupid, can still lord it over us in camp—because we're always hungry and dirty."

He puffed deeply, regarding the cigar and his fingernails in turn. Then he said softly: "Excuse me," and cleaned his nails with a broken matchstick. "There, now I almost feel good . . . almost." He gazed intently into the chaplain's eyes, and a trace of sympathy appeared on his face. "I really don't know what you're so annoyed about." The chaplain rose with a jerk, as if a fire had started under him; he paced agitatedly in front of the bookcases, his face an odd mixture of fear, sorrow, indignation, and uncertainty.

"In fact," Joseph continued, when he received no answer, "I'm the one who could be offended, since you're not offering me any wine. And viewed objectively, I am a rather charming fellow."

The chaplain paused abruptly before him and stammered: "Are you . . . are you . . . a criminal?"

Joseph's eyes narrowed and hardened; he looked at him searchingly. "Of course, I committed a crime against the state, and I think you're about to as well." He glanced at the scattered pages of the manuscript covering the desk. "That is, if you truly represent the ideas that your uniform stands for."

"You let me worry about that." The chaplain laughed, apparently trying to salvage a little humor from the situation. Joseph asked again about wine, but the chaplain merely smiled uncertainly, then paled in fear and nearly cried aloud as Joseph stepped up to him, cowering defensively as Joseph seized him by the top button of his soutane. "All right," he said softly, very softly, "I'll get you some wine."

But Joseph threw his cigar angrily down on the desk and released his hold. "Oh"—he waved him off wearily—"if you only understood what wine it is I want from you. What good do all these treasures do you?" He gestured roughly at the books. "You've learned as little from them as your *confrères* fifty years ago learned from the fulsome pandects we find so contemptible today. . . ." He struck the bookcase dully with his fist. Then he hesitated as he saw the chaplain's tortured face, but his words gushed like a spring released by a drill. "You soak in your certainties like a man in a bathtub of lukewarm water, indecisive, hardly daring to get out and dry off. But you forget that the water is turning cold according to inexorable laws, as cold as reality." His voice had lost its accusatory tone and was almost imploring. He released his gaze from the shocked face of the chaplain and ran his eyes over the book titles. "Here," he said sadly. "You wanted to know my crime." And he threw the slim brochure onto the desk: "There it is . . . and now, good-bye." He took a deep breath and looked around the room a final time, then knelt and said softly: "Bless me, Father, I have a dangerous road ahead." The priest folded his hands and made the sign of the cross over him, and as he tried to hold him back with a helpless smile, Joseph said quietly: "No, forgive me. . . . I have to go now, my life is at stake." And before he left the house, he made the sign of cross over the figure in black.

It was now totally dark outside, as if the night had rolled itself into a tight ball. The village seemed to cower in darkness, like a flock in a gloomy cave, swallowed by brute silence. It seemed as if loneliness braced itself icily against Joseph as he wended his way cautiously through the dark alleys to the open fields. As if in final farewell, the bells of the church rang in consolation through the night. Four times they sounded from the tower, bright and almost joyful, then twice, dark and heavy, as if God's hammer were falling through all eternity.

In the silent gloom the tones were like a reminder to hold fast to his faith.

Soon he could distinguish the ground's surface and larger obstacles, hedges and bushes and ditches. He could go only by sixth sense, instinctively following the street, which angled away toward the country road. He felt almost nothing, his heart heavy with silence, the infinite silence of one who suffers, for whom there is no answer under the heavens, no answer but God's promise, spanning the earth, wherever any person suffers for the sake of the cross. He was so far, so far from all hate and all bitterness, that prayers formed in him like pure, steady flames rising from the garden of faith, hope, and love, innocent and beautiful as flowers.

He crossed a wooded area, feeling his way cautiously from tree to tree to keep from stumbling in the darkness. Emerging into the open, he saw lights. To the right, ghostly and distant, rose tall structures, illuminated by yellow light, steel-ribbed skeletons. Behind them glowed the red jaws of the blast furnaces, like the gullet of the underworld. My God, those must be the factories at Gordelen! The border lay just beyond them. It couldn't be more than a half hour away. The field fell away before him and was bordered by a line of trees, their silhouette outlined against the distant light, and he saw how the trees ran on ahead, far across the dark, level fields, toward the factory. It must be a road. Everything beyond it lay in darkness; a thick forest seemed to extend into the distance, perhaps even beyond the border.

Nothing could be heard but the strange, distant, grinding murmur from the blast furnaces and pits.

The field before him appeared smooth, a treeless meadow without bushes. He headed to the left, but there was no cover that would allow him to reach the road. He hesitated, saw with increasing clarity the motionless line of trees on the dark base of the road, like an endless row of teeth. Fear overwhelmed him again, tugging violently and mockingly at the cloak of his self-composure. He seemed to see the monstrous grin of a bestial mouth stretched across the face of the night. He pushed off from the tree, almost violently, and began to run. The steep meadow seemed to swallow him; he hadn't realized how abruptly it would fall away.

Suddenly, the heavens seemed to split in two, and the dazzling beam of a searchlight shot out in front of him, as if he had brought it to life. He fell to the ground as if struck by lightning, landing painfully on his chin. His face pressed deep into the bitter, cool damp of the earth while the searchlight sailed back and forth over him like a huge yellow whip. With his face in the soil he failed to hear the sentry's challenge, then a burst of fire raced like an apocalyptic gurgle across the earth in front of him, the bullets thudding into the ground. He lay there, nailed fast by the murderous light, like a target set on the meadow's slope. And before the next series of shots ripped through him he screamed, screamed so loudly in his forsakenness that the heavens would surely collapse. He raised his head again and screamed, blinded by the light, before a final burst from the snarling muzzle extinguished his cries.

All was still as his tormentors surrounded him, shining their flashlights on his torn body, which resembled the earth so closely that it might have been the earth itself that bled. "Yes . . . that's him," said an indifferent voice.

Youth on Fire

HEINRICH PERKONING WAS SIXTEEN YEARS old when, for the first time, he felt like dying. On a gray December day, strolling through the large city he called home, he saw an elderly gentleman he knew follow a bold young prostitute into her house. He was overwhelmed by such infinite pain that he wanted to die. The anguish he felt, which seemed immeasurable, increased with each passing day. He saw so many ugly and evil things, and so few that gave joy to his soul, that he decided to kill himself. He didn't say a word to anyone. He suffered for a year, and no one sensed his pain. He was often on the verge of confiding in someone he thought he could trust but always recoiled at the merely superficial interest they showed, and he closed his heart.

Now he was walking—on yet another December day—along the bank of a broad river, thinking of only one thing: killing himself, taking his own life. Trembling, he slowly descended the stone steps leading to the water. He paused on the bottom step. The water lapped intimately at the stones, as if in gentle encouragement. He'd planned everything carefully in advance: He would drape his coat loosely around his shoulders and sew it up tightly from the inside, preventing any possible swimming motion. He thought again with a shudder of all those who would suffer at the nature and manner of his death. His mother and father, his siblings, and a few others, friends, one or two young women among them, who thought they loved him. They all passed through his mind, slowly and silently. A scarcely perceptible wave of love and longing rose in him yet could not hold him back. He had struggled far too often against such feelings. And he saw the face of a suffering young priest, whispering to him, "The Son of Man knew not where to lay his head, so forsaken was he, so miserable and forsaken among men. Even his disciples deserted him in his hour of need. Only the power of the Holy Spirit could have given them strength to bear the terrible agony and pain, for the sake of God. And yet the Son of Man still loved them. He knew how ugly and evil the world was, but he was filled with love for a mankind that had strayed—and gave his life for them, and for you. If you believe in him—as you've always claimed—then follow his example and love them all, the bad, those who have lost their way, all those who suffer." Heinrich trembled violently and groaned: "I can't bear it!" But a voice within him, more powerful than he had ever heard, roared: "God's mercy and love flow everywhere; have faith in Him!" And Heinrich turned and ascended the stairs.

He walked along the broad passage beneath the arch of the bridge. Across the street stood a brightly painted wooden pavilion surrounded by shrubs and small trees, a disreputable café. Heinrich reached in his pocket, counted his money, and crossed the street. He entered the grimy place and sat down wordlessly in one of several booths surrounding a small dance floor. An aged, slovenly waitress brought the coffee he ordered. The walls were decorated with stylized red nudes. Lecherous men of various ages sat about with prostitutes. A pretty young girl around seventeen years old, dressed like a prostitute, sat down beside him. She smiled strangely as he waved her away with a tired gesture. Heinrich took out the New Testament he always carried and began to read. The young woman's eyes were so striking he trembled in confusion. He tried to concentrate on the text, but kept glancing into her smiling eyes, which were staring fixedly at him. She propped her elbows on the table and put her chin in her hands. Her brown hair was soft and thick, her face clever and charming, her eyes pure and beautiful, almost childlike. At first Heinrich viewed her with mistrust, but with each glance he grew more surprised. Her large, dark eyes were filled with sorrow; they were pure like those of a child, and sad like those of . . . But she's a prostitute all the same, he thought, she's trying to seduce me, I must be wrong, she's no good. He returned to his reading. Still, he felt compelled to keep looking up, until, no longer able to bear the terrible uncertainty, he asked in a harsh, brusque voice: "What are you doing here?" She seemed to have been waiting for this question. She loosened a chain with a crucifix from her neck and said in a firm, clear voice, pointing to the cross: "I come in the name of this sign."

Heinrich looked down and blushed in confusion. "I don't really understand, but I believe you." The young woman smiled gently and continued: "Let me explain; it's really quite simple. I've taken a job in this . . . place . . . as a prostitute—you know about such things—on a rescue mission. I want to save people, and since I don't think I'm strong enough to battle with lecherous older men, I'm trying to save the young ones. There are countless young men on the verge of ruin. You're not the first I've approached under the mask of sin, but of those I've joined, you're the first who didn't need my help." Heinrich gazed at her speechlessly, as if he couldn't believe his ears. Beneath his almost enraptured gaze, she turned serious and her smile faltered. Now that the sadness in her eyes was no longer muted by her smile, he could see clearly into the bottomless depths of sorrow in her soul.

He wanted to ask if she'd saved anyone yet, but was ashamed to demand an accounting, and waited for her to continue. She sat in mystical beauty, leaning forward slightly, with the suffering visage of an apocalyptic angel. Heinrich could tell that something strange and unexpected was taking place inside her, and in a powerful new rush of shame he covered his face with his hands. All at once he loved this young woman. She continued, her voice now trembling with excitement: "I actually managed to save one of them. He came stumbling in the first week I was here. I could tell he wasn't drunk, but simply weak from hunger. He was as pale as death, his black hair unkempt, and yet he lived. He sat down and shouted almost madly for a woman. I took his arm and led him to my room to save him from scorn, for I could see he was practically insane with misery. I gave him something to eat and let him tell his story. Then he fell asleep.

"I sat beside him for a long time, making sure no one disturbed him. When he awoke he demanded something of me, but fell silent at my look. Then I spoke to him. He was as stunned as a heathen by what I told him. He left early that morning. He visited me often, wanting to hear more about Christ. He hasn't been here for the past four months. He's ashamed of something. I felt it the last time he was here. He wanted to tell me something, but was too ashamed. I know his name, but not his address. I'd like to visit him."

When she finished speaking, she seemed to collapse, sinking down on the table and covering her face with both hands, weeping. Heinrich bent over her. The pain of his love was forgotten; he wanted only to help. "I'll find him, I promise, I . . . I . . ." She straightened up and looked at him with a burning, tear-filled gaze. "I think you . . . you . . . may have misunderstood me. . . ." She looked at him so strangely that he suddenly knew with utmost clarity that she loved him, not the runaway he had offered to find. He bent down to the weeping girl and whispered: "Don't cry, be happy; help me celebrate the new life I've been granted. I'll serve you, I'll love you more than life itself, please don't cry. We'll leave this squalor and begin a Christian life of poverty. We . . ." He felt such joy that words failed him. Language, the most awkward of human mediators, was incapable of expressing what his soul felt. He sank down and kissed the girl's hands. She trembled with joy as he lifted her up and took her in his arms.

That same evening Susanne left her "job." Heinrich sought a place for her to live in the city. She rented a small, clean room where they sat late into the night gazing at each other, but speaking little. They decided to visit Benedikt Tauster, the only person Susanne had managed to save in the torment of her stay at the brothel. Benedikt Tauster was eighteen years old when he first drew public attention. He wrote the infamous essay, "Was Napoleon an Erotic Genius as Well?!" subtitled "Meditations on the Well-Known Charmer from Corsica." Even the exclamation mark after the question enraged some readers, although their rage no longer boiled but had now been distilled as steam. Heinrich heard about Benedikt Tauster from one of those readers who had disliked the article. He read his essay and found that its scorn and mockery were directed with almost satanic intelligence against the present situation, for although the text discussed Napoleon's erotic life, it dealt primarily with the contemporary world. The political and social parallels were often so clever that Heinrich laughed till he cried. What impressed him most, however, was the fervent tone that permeated the essay, a wild, intense rapture, which fascinated precisely because it was coupled with irony. The tract concluded like a child apologizing for some naughty deed: "It's too bad that I, Benedikt Tauster, am such a hopeless cripple."

Heinrich discovered Benedikt's whereabouts indirectly, by way of a famous man of letters who had a reputation as a brilliant literary critic. This man had once stated, "Dostoyevsky's greatness lies in the fact that he was a truly gifted disciple of Goethe." As a result of this pronouncement, three shots were fired at his laurel-laden head. Heinrich learned about him through a prison guard. While paying a pedagogical visit to the man who had made the attempt on his estimable life, the critic whispered in the prison guard's ear: "Unless I'm greatly mistaken—and I doubt that I am—you'll probably be seeing this fellow Benedikt Tauster before long, too." The prison guard, who knew Heinrich, told him about Benedikt Tauster, since he knew that Heinrich had "literary" interests.

Heinrich found Benedikt living in a run-down garret in a bad part of town. He was tall and very thin, with a pale, tormented face. When Heinrich introduced himself as Susanne's fiancé and said they had been looking for him, Benedikt regarded him silently for some time. Then, in a quiet but congenial tone, he said: "So we're friends." Heinrich nodded, and their friendship began. They sat silently for some time, smoking. Then Benedikt looked up and said quietly: "You believe in Christ." Heinrich said: "Yes," although it had not been put as a question. "You've surely read my essay on Napoleon. You know, those swine, those constipated penmen, simply left out the opening. I began 'May God forgive me if my essay is unworthy. I wrote it in anger at those who make a mockery of His name, yet call themselves Christians.' And they left that out." He looked at Heinrich with flashing eyes.

Benedikt stood and paced the room in thought for some time, then finally came to a stop before Heinrich and said: "I'd like to ask you something." He paused and seemed to be considering whether or not to continue. "In six months a young woman you'll soon meet will bear my child. I met her in a pawnshop. I'd gone there early in the morning, to pawn the only thing I had of value, my watch, because I hadn't eaten for days. I passed it across the counter, the watch was appraised, everything was fine, I was to receive five marks. Then the man asked to see my papers. . . . Embarrassed, I stammered that I didn't have any. He passed the watch back to me and I was about to leave shamefaced when I heard the clear voice of a young woman behind me: 'I'll vouch for the gentleman; here's my identity card.'

"I turned in surprise and looked at her as she handed him her card. She was about my height, with dark hair and a pale face. She regarded me with serious, dark eyes. The man returned her card: 'In the first place you can't offer security for someone else, and secondly you're not an adult yourself, so I can't take your things either.'

"I took her arm and accompanied her home. I was astonished at how naturally everything came to me. I'd never escorted a young woman before. We talked and talked, and were friends at once. I didn't fall in love with her; I simply loved her. As we walked we even cheered up and joked about how hungry we were. But for the most part she walked silently beside me, in melancholy sadness. Only occasionally did she show a spark of joy, saying something with a smile. Her smile was charming, the bright, full-blooded smile of a young woman. We said good-bye on a street corner. I told her where I lived and invited her to come see me. She said nothing, but came that very evening.

"When she arrived, I went straight to her and kissed her. She smiled again. She dropped by every evening, and we would sit and talk. First we recounted our lives, then talked about everything, about God, art, politics—it was wonderful listening to her clever words. And then we prayed together. We revered the good thief crucified at Christ's side, who joined him that very day in paradise.

"My financial affairs were going from bad to worse back then. My only regular income was the twenty-five marks I received each month from the executor of my small inheritance. It had reached a point where I could no longer afford the bare necessities, like clothes and shoes. I started several projects, but the Napoleon essay was the only one I finished. I entrusted it to her, and she carried it around to various houses for almost three weeks, until she found someone willing to publish it. A publisher's representative visited me (a publisher who'd made a fortune with trashy novels). We quickly reached an agreement.

"It was around this time that her father committed suicide. He was a businessman who'd managed to keep his head above water by a series of clever maneuvers, in spite of being deeply in debt. Now his shady deals had been discovered, and he shot himself. She came to me late that afternoon. I longed to see her, for I was sad, even through I had signed a relatively advantageous contract. In the powerful heat of the late summer day, heavy storm clouds were forming on the horizon. The sun had just set, and I gazed from my small window across a city drenched in red. It looked less forlorn than normal . . . and yet I felt I could die of sorrow, and knew how much I needed her. Then she arrived, looking half insane. She collapsed into my arms, and gradually I pieced together what had happened from the phrases she stammered out. I could think of nothing to say, and kissed her wordlessly. That night she stayed with me. And that day . . . we lost our innocence."

Benedikt talked rapidly, pacing back and forth. Now he broke off and stared out the window. Heinrich wanted to go to him, say something, at least press his hand, when the dark figure of a young woman entered. He recognized her immediately from his description. He greeted her, and Benedikt introduced them. Benedikt gave her his chair and sat beside Heinrich on the bed. In the dim light of the room the two youths could barely make out her silhouette. She began speaking softly in a warm voice: "I've found something for you. A gentleman who runs a private school afternoons is looking for someone to teach grammar-school subjects part time for one mark an hour. You'd have to teach middle-class children who haven't done well in school. The work would be steady, six or seven hours a day. There's a short qualifying exam, but the gentleman waived it. I spoke with him, told him you already have a grammar-school degree. He gets three marks an hour from the parents, by the way." Benedikt looked up slowly: "Thank you, Magdalena. . . . That means we can get married, that is . . . if God . . ."

All three sat for a long time in the half-darkness. Only once was the silence broken, by Benedikt: "Magdalena, I told you about the young woman in the brothel who taught me the truth about things, you remember. . . . She's to be Heinrich's bride. . . ."

Magdalena sprang up, went over to Heinrich, and fixed her unusually large, dark eyes somberly upon him: "Has she forgiven him . . . forgiven us . . . for not returning to her? We were too ashamed to face her purity." She turned bright red and stared at the floor. When she looked up again she saw Heinrich smile and nod. She pulled up her chair and joined them.

While Magdalena stayed with Susanne, almost joyful in the aura of the latter's glowing faith, the two youths visited the capitalist schoolmaster. The cold winter rain that murders the poor was still falling. Hatless, clad only in their thin, threadbare coats, they stuck close to the walls of the buildings as they walked along, accepting what little protection they offered. On a broad and elegant suburban avenue, where houses lay in studied reserve behind rows of tall trees and garden parks, they rang the bell of an almost palatial home. They were led into a reception area and left waiting for over an hour. After tracing the origin and history of every picture in the room angrily and in sarcastic detail, they were almost in a frenzy, and were about to turn their attention to the wallpaper pattern when a "serious" gentleman entered. He was of average height and portly build, with the smile of a Buddha. They introduced themselves; he greeted them amiably and within five minutes, without an exam, Benedikt was hired on the basis of his degree for a probationary period of one month. Heinrich said he would like to teach as well, and after a quick glance at his credentials he was taken on, in spite of his youth. "You can start this afternoon," and with these words they were dismissed. They returned along the same barren route.

"The man is either stupid or crazy," said Heinrich. "He's risking the entire reputation of his famous school, hiring us just like that."

Benedikt laughed: "He's not crazy, but he is too lazy. But he's not stupid either. Since he knows Magdalena he probably realizes we're Catholic, and believers. Catholics, he figures, are afraid to commit a sin, since they know they'll have to go through the humiliation of confession. They cheat less than those who don't have to slip into a box at regular intervals to unburden their souls. . . . There are plenty of unbelievers who will only hire Catholic maids, you know, because they think they won't dare steal anything for fear of having to confess. And he can toss us out anytime he thinks we're endangering his reputation."

Magdalena was still with Susanne. It was pleasant sitting beside the warm stove, drinking hot coffee and smoking.

Benedikt and Magdalena soon took their leave, since they still had to see the priest about their wedding, which was to take place in a week.

Susanne sat beside Heinrich. He stared into her eyes: "Susanne, I've always hated the sun because I thought its blissful rays were mocking my pain. I found it hard to live, let alone feel any pleasure in life. Then one day I found the will to live, and that same day I found you, the joy of my life. The sun hasn't shone since that day, in punishment for my blasphemy, but it will surely appear again, and I'll greet it joyfully. The days will be filled with wonder for us, Susanne . . . Susanne. . . ." He smiled, the first smile Susanne had seen upon his face, like the simple, clear, godly music of ancient times tentatively settling upon his young countenance. Susanne was happy to see this gentle outbreak of joy. They shared something so pure, so far from sin—in an era so constantly near it—that it resembled medieval courtly love, a pleasant, tender breath of blessedness, full of silent jubilation. Heinrich drew her gently closer, kissed her mouth, and the earth seemed to vanish beneath their feet.

The wedding was as sad as a child's funeral. The majestic cathedral, infinitely vast and lofty, had no doubt rarely witnessed a ceremony so forlorn. The few poorly clothed people kneeling before a side altar seemed crushed to pitiful insignificance by the huge room, whose high ceiling of disintegrating gray resembled the cloudy February sky. Magdalena closed her eyes humbly, trembling with joy as she awaited the holy sacrament of marriage, and when, in the course of the ceremony, the priest turned, it was Benedikt's pale, earnest face he confronted. Magdalena's mother and brothers knelt behind them. Her mother's face bore a hint of painful submission, like a violated maiden who, in the purity of her soul, is beginning to forget her body's shame. Something of her brothers' debauchery could still be read in their eyes, masked by their boldness. It was no doubt they who, along with her father, had violated the soul of this woman. From time to time they would sneak a glance at Susanne, kneeling before them at Magdalena's side, her head bowed. The two witnesses, Heinrich and Paul von Sentau, assisted at the mass.

After the benediction the couple stepped forward and knelt on the ancient, plain hassock that had served in many a princely wedding. Both witnesses joined them and the priest began. When the holy ceremony was completed, the young priest spoke. He spoke softly, as if he were afraid of awaking an echo in that vast space, a smile of joy on his face.

"It's customary for the priest to say a few words to a young couple upon uniting them in holy matrimony. Please forgive me, but I can't speak at the moment. . . . We so seldom see true Christian feeling and humbleness before God these days. I hope you understand." He blushed and looked at the floor. "I'm too deeply moved. . . . But permit me to accept your invitation to a small celebration."

Magdalena's brothers took their leave in front of the cathedral. With the disappearance of their greedy, nasty faces, a sense of oppression seemed to lift from the pitifully small party. They walked through the daily life of the great city to their new apartment, situated near the outskirts of the old part of town. The cathedral wasn't actually in their parish, but Benedikt wanted to be married there because that was where his parents had been married, and where he himself had been baptized. The young priest to whom he'd opened his glowing heart six months ago, the night he received the spark of divine truth from Susanne, had gone through old church records and discovered that Danile Tauster had been joined in matrimony with one Adelheid von Sentau in the second year of the Great War. Benedikt's baptism was also recorded. So now they had a fairly long walk from the city center to the suburbs. The young couple led the way, conversing quietly. Magdalena's mother followed with the priest. Susanne walked behind them, between Heinrich and Paul.

Paul, who'd never met Susanne before, was telling her about himself: "I'm the last descendant of a noble Frankish family reduced to middle-class circumstances over a hundred years ago. My cousin Benedikt is my only blood relative. I was born the day my father fell at Langemarck. My mother was barely eighteen. Her young husband's love had rescued her from an orphan's painful life, and she was devastated by his death. Benedikt's mother, my father's sister, only nineteen herself, took me in when I was six months old, although she was expecting a child and deeply concerned about her husband, hospitalized in Romania with a serious head injury. Her husband died three months before Benedikt was born. She bore the sorrow over her husband, her brother, and my mother along with the infinite burden of life. She forced her fiery young soul through the business of everyday life, believing in Christ, the herald of truth and the friend of all those who suffer.

"She received scant pleasure from the boys she raised. She

was forced to get a job, and we spent our long morning hours with Veit, a crippled veteran, who lived in a garret next to us. Veit had lost a leg, and had a hard time climbing all those steps on his crutches. He spent a lot of time in bed because his lungs were bad, and he was glad to have us around since he was still young. He was thirty-two years old, and full of energy, and when he learned that our fathers had died in the Great War, he came to love us.

"I was five, Benedikt not quite four, when our friendship with Veit began. Veit believed in nothing. When we entered his room, he would ask with mock solemnity: 'What is the basic rule of life?' and our high-pitched children's voices would respond according to his teaching, 'Everything is shit!' He'd lived through terrible times, and told us horror stories, which we found fascinating. He dripped the poison of unbelief into our childish souls, which remained untouched by the prayers we said each evening when our mother came home, weary and kind. Veit wasn't a bad man, but he had lost touch with God. I think now that the Holy Ghost stirred mysteriously within him, for on one of the final days of his life—I was seven at the time—he said: 'Boys, what do you say in your evening prayers?' 'We pray to Jesus Christ to protect our souls from unbelief, to take our fathers to heaven, to make Veit well again, and to grant our mother happiness.' He smiled uncertainly at us and said: 'That's good, don't forget to say them.' This remark, which ran counter to all his wisdom over the past two years, was to us simply one impression among thousands; we merely absorbed them without differentiating.

"Veit died a few days later. We mourned him deeply for a long time. Mother tried in vain to console us. Time alone healed this wound, and after a period of mourning, the seeds he'd sown began to sprout. We contradicted our mother when she spoke of things in which—as far as we recalled—Veit had not believed, although we did not yet doubt God. That happened much later, when we were exposed to the corrupt wisdom of the streets, and when, after our mother's death, we were despised in high school by the sons of the middle-class and newly wealthy upstarts because we were poor. Increasingly isolated within the realm of our own minds, slowly at first, then with startling suddenness, we denied all things metaphysical, bearing our poverty proudly with bitter, pale faces. We were awash in skepticism, and circumstances and our own shortsightedness conspired to turn us from the cross—repulsed by the cripples who called themselves Christians—long before we knew the first thing about its teachings.

"Our mother died when I was nine, and Benedikt barely eight. The doctors said she died from overwork. She had surely been weakened by the drudgery she undertook out of love for us, but I believe, in fact I'm sure, that she died of sorrow. It had fermented in her for years, and at last dealt her a devastating blow which sent her into the eternal life in which she had always believed. Had she offered us the gentle teachings of the cross in those decisive early years we surely would have understood, and would not have foundered upon the ignorance and shortcomings of the world around us. Instead we were forced to wander aimlessly for years on end, groping blindly. We lived on the proceeds of a tiny house Benedikt's mother had purchased with her scanty income to offer some small security for the future. People talk about magnificent memorials, documents of love. For me nothing compares to that tiny, crooked old house in the old city, for which a beautiful, tormented, lonely young woman suffered long years of hunger.

"One year before my final high school exam, I left Benedikt and my hometown for the sake of a woman. She had dark brown hair, a splendid young mouth, and eyes black as night, burning with fire. She gave a Chopin concert back then. . . . I listened in a trance—moved for the first time in my life, inspired by the music's magical, melancholy, seductive sensuality. This young woman, whose profound performance filled my soul with ecstasy, became my sole desire. The applause still sounded through the thick curtains as I waited in her dressing room. Her lackeys had withdrawn under my gaze, the curtain was pulled back, and she entered with noiseless grace. She was neither startled nor angry. Without noticing that I was dressed like a beggar, she looked into my eyes and smiled. She was very young, seventeen. I saw at once that she was still as innocent as I was. She stood for some time, smiling, while I waited, pale with pain and joy. She approached and kissed me. I had never kissed a woman before, and felt the joy of that first kiss from a woman I loved. In a soft voice that made me tremble, she said: 'I know you'll laugh, but I love you. You're my first and only love.' We were united in a night filled with dizzying, sweet pleasure—joyful, but lacking God's blessing.

"I traveled the world with her that year. She gave concerts, was famous. . . . Never in all that time did I have any clothes other than this old worn school uniform. She never noticed such things; she was natural and warm, and I didn't think about them either. We never went to parties. We were always alone,

alone with our youth, our love. I could never bring myself to attend one of her concerts; those thousands of eager eyes trained on her body, which was mine, would have driven me insane.

"Neither one of us thought about Christ, but a guardian angel hovered over us, and we were never base. My existence did not remain unnoticed. The press had discovered me; I know the journalists referred to me among themselves as the great pianist's gigolo. We sinned greatly, but every day was as fresh, glowing, and joyful as the first. And the pleas of my mother, who saw the fruit of her young womb enmeshed in sin, and the entreaties of my second mother at God's throne, were not in vain. . . . I found my way back.

"I was out walking one evening in some small town or other in southern Germany while she was giving a concert, my heart still on fire from our parting, which had taken place before the eyes of the local squire—and all at once it was clear to me that I was taking unfair advantage of her, allowing her to work for me, for I had long since realized that she was miserable playing before the audiences she faced. Only when we were alone, only when she opened her burning heart to me on the piano or violin, was music a joy to her. The realization struck me with terrible force.

"I fled to a nearby church because I knew it was the only place where I could be alone and sat in a back row of the church, shrouded in darkness. The softly murmured prayer reached my ears faintly above the voices of the sparse congregation as they sang. Then I was startled by a loud, clear voice: 'Every sin, every offense against God, begins in pride, even in the slightest arrogance toward a neighbor.' An elderly priest had mounted the pulpit to deliver the sermon, and I was forced to listen, first by his loud, clear voice, and then by what he was saying. My mind followed his words as if entranced, and within a scant fifteen minutes I heard what seemed a strikingly clear overview of the doctrine of the cross. He spoke of humility, of love, of virtue, and when he spoke of ordination, of order, of divine measure, I winced. I realized I had offended against the divine order; it struck me like a bolt of lightning. I was so totally downcast I didn't hear what followed, and remained alone in the church at the conclusion of devotions. I sat for a long time, sweating in agony, and thought I was going to die. I heard footsteps in the silence, looked up, and saw the priest, who, having genuflected before the tabernacle, was preparing to leave. I waved to him like a drowning man. When he stood beside me, regarding me with solemn goodwill, I found I couldn't speak. I saw, believed in, felt God only vaguely, but nonetheless truly. I suffered terribly for my sins, yet I knew as never before that Natalie was a sublime creature of God, and that she was not wicked. I begged God to move her heart as mine had been with the truth and clarity of his being. Then, my voice weak, I spoke to the priest, and told him everything.

"On the way back to the hotel the joy of divine truth burst upon me, and I burned to pass on this treasure, the only one worth possessing, to the person I loved . . . still loved. I had no doubt that she would understand. I knew she had natural longings, for I recalled the many hours she wept hot tears because our love remained childless. And her art revealed there was more in her than mere nature. Walking through that late night I seemed to hear again her thousand passionate fantasias, and they were not reduced to vapid meaninglessness when measured by my Christian conscience. I rejoiced in the blissful expectation of showing her the goal. You'll soon learn how things turned out. You'll see a young woman, in many ways still a girl, wearing a plain gold band on her right finger, the symbol of our union. She will be wearing a simple red dress, her only jewelry a rosary, the prayer book of the humble . . . the great pianist who married her gigolo and became Natalie von Sentau."

Paul beamed at the two of them, having kept his eyes on the pavement throughout his story. Susanne glowed confusedly over this strange young man, who had no doubt read in her eyes that she would understand him. She saw that Heinrich was smiling.

The small party was received at the door by a slender young woman with brown hair, wearing a simple, dark red dress. The dark beads and gold cross of a rosary were visible about her neck. She had strikingly large, dark eyes, a delicately curved nose. She greeted the young couple first, kissing Magdalena and taking Heinrich's hand firmly. Paul came over quickly and introduced her to the priest and Susanne: "Here she is," he said to Susanne with a laugh.

Natalie had prepared a fine breakfast. The table was tastefully set, there were flowers everywhere, and in the corner a candle burned before a picture of the Virgin Mary.

Natalie smiled as she noticed the surprised looks on their faces: "I discovered it only this morning, in the attic of an old house, looking like a shapeless clump of dust. Who knows how many owners of that tiny house had shoved it aside without noticing it. At first I thought it was a dusty old distaff, but when I lifted it up, it was very heavy, and wherever I touched it gold shimmered through. . . . It must be very old.

A delicious aroma of coffee filled the room. Bread too stood on the table, enticing brown and hearty black, with yellow butter in a brown dish. They sat down happily. February had turned somewhat friendlier, the gray sky at least empty of threatening rain clouds, and a weak glimmer of sun came in through the window from the southwest. It was still cold outside, but here in the room it was pleasantly warm. They spoke little as they ate; something akin to respect for the newly sanctified couple reigned over them.

When they had finished eating, the coffee cups were refilled and tendrils of blue tobacco smoke began to fill the room. Paul said: "We need to think a few things over." Everyone looked at him expectantly. He smiled. "Surely you can see we have to form some sort of club or alliance—something of that kind."

"I agree," Heinrich said, as the others laughed. "Whenever three or more people are in general agreement, something should be set up with membership cards and dues. It would be a strange club, all right: eight members to begin with: a young man crazy enough to get married on a monthly income of less than two hundred marks; the wife of this idiot, who has thereby dropped out of the middle class; the mother of that deranged person; then a great artist who resigned her calling, whose husband, leading a nomadic existence, is the last of his line, a totally degenerate descendant of an ancient noble family; a priest totally enslaved by the Catholic Church; Susanne with her slightly more than shady past; and me. . . ."

"If I can chair the group and compose the club song, I'll join up," said Benedikt, puffing on his pipe with a smile.

The conversation would no doubt have continued in this vein for some time had not the young priest, who had been smiling as he listened, now raised his right hand to stem the tide, speaking softly, almost into the pipe he had just lighted: "In all things truly ridiculous—and of course few of the things people tend to make fun of actually are—one finds something twisted, crooked, or false—and so the ridiculous always has its serious, even satanic, side as well. Clubs, for example, are usually ridiculous, yet still, if they turn truly false and ridiculous, they prove to be no more than one of the thousand various shades of the divine service. I'm convinced many club members who attend church regularly and are 'good Christians' would be far more upset, perhaps even stirred to revolutionary action in spite of their normal apathy, if one of their club rules were broken—or the club funds misused—far more upset than they would be if a sentence were to be struck from the Credo. That's only by way of an example. Whether these things are called current fashion, sports, dance, exercise, or the cinema—or, as is most often the case, money—they are generally nothing more than well-laid, almost comfortably middle-class traps set by Satan. He consumes the still healthy core within them, using them—in nice, decent middle-class fashion (most people are too lazy, tired, and dull to sin wildly)—to divert people gradually from the truth—or better yet, from the tiny residue of truth that would have saved them. And when things have finally reached the point where even those whose duty it is to protect the truth support such traps, then things take their natural course: Beauty is derided, the feeling for beauty is corroded, desire is whipped into a frenzy. It's easy to brew a vile broth from such swamps. So if someone truly wants to found a new club, it should be a 'Club for the Friends of the Absolute.' But that already exists. . . . It's called the Church."

He smiled at his strange conclusion. The others had fallen into thoughtful silence. The young men smoked quietly, thinking to themselves. The young women gazed straight ahead. Magdalena's mother looked at the priest, slightly surprised. Susanne rose and relighted the candle standing before the Madonna, which had somehow gone out. Natalie said softly: "I'd like to play something"—she blushed—"if you . . ." Everyone nodded. She stood up and asked Heinrich, who was sitting by the bookcase, to pass her the music. "Beethoven," she said, as he looked at her inquiringly. And while the men laid aside their pipes, and sunlight suddenly streamed through the window, Natalie stepped to the piano, which stood against a white wall unadorned by pictures, bearing only a large black cross.

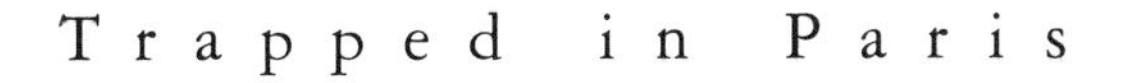

Trapped in Paris

REINHARD PLUNDERED THE PAYMASTER'S bullet-riddled car with a soldier's cool indifference. The last stragglers had long since disappeared into the various streets spread out fanlike from the square, and there was no sound or sight of the enemy. The park, ripped and torn by shells, brooded in desolate silence, and the facades of the buildings gaped like an eerily empty stage. Here and there curtains fluttered wildly, almost longingly, from the windows; you could almost hear the frightened breath of people hiding in the cellars, not daring to trust the uncanny stillness in the aftermath of the roar of the attack. The semicircle of the square that adjoined the park—the central portion of the fan from which streets radiated like slender, elegant spokes—was strewn with steel helmets, gas masks, and broken rifles. A bright, smiling heaven arched auspiciously above the incomparably beautiful city, whose brilliance and loveliness beckoned from each of its countless windows. And between scraps of military equipment on the soft, saturated, deep green stretches of grass furrowed with trenches lay corpses, corpses in gray uniforms. It was like a lull in a revolution where the center of action had shifted to some other part of the city, drawing all life along with it. And while the corpses on the meadow clasped the earth as if frozen in eternal lament, the trees that lined the avenue trembled beneath the lighthearted caresses of the soft summer breeze.

Reinhard had slung his weapon and his gear beside the disabled vehicle and was rummaging through a jumble of cardboard boxes, discovering delicacies he had not seen in the long, long years of war. Marvelous cigars and soaps whose mere fragrance could have spelled peace, chocolates and biscuits, the finest linens. With startling rapidity he pulled off his filthy, sweat-soaked shirt and felt the pleasure of a new silk one against his body. He then stuffed his pockets systematically, cramming in as much as he could, intoxicated with happiness, digging through the riches at random, sensing with wild delight that the war, which had seemed so cruel and endless, was beginning to unravel. It was inevitably dissolving, dispersing like a gray, persistent pall of cloud scattered by golden flicks of the sun's lash; the war was unraveling. It seemed to Reinhard as if a huge steel cover screwed down airtight over him had suddenly lifted, releasing him into light and air, and he breathed deeply with a wild, powerful sense of freedom. He drew on his magnificent cigar with a smile, released a blue cloud of smoke into the splendid air, and thought of his wife. Soon he would see her again, soon life would begin, and with a laugh he tossed a couple of packs of cigarettes back in the car to make room for a few bars of expensive soap, fit for a princess, for his sweet love. Then he bent to pick up his sword belt and fasten it around his stuffed and swollen waist. But the next moment he lay flattened against the hot, smelly asphalt, breathing heavily.

From a small grove across the park came a whole column of diminutive, fast-moving cars with soldiers in khaki uniforms, careening madly in a broad front, firing blindly as they approached the square. The last remnant of stillness disappeared as a bullet shattered the car's windshield above him. Gripped suddenly by fear, he was unable to take a calm look to his rear; his confused eyes saw only the merciless smooth surface of the square, across which no flight was possible. The small khaki cars had reached the avenue, gathering on the semicircular square like a pack of small, agile, barking dogs, then dispersing into the streets. One of them passed within a hair's breadth of Reinhard's head, but he had long since assumed the crumpled position he had so often seen among the dead, warding off and embracing in a single gesture. The contented growl of well-maintained tanks approached from the park, and now, risking a quick glance past the flat tire, he saw the advancing columns of infantry and knew it was time to act. The war machine was descending upon him like a cruel curtain and somewhere far beyond it, where the streets opened outward like canyons of deliverance, was the small, beloved face of his wife.

He rose to his knees, concealed behind the bullet-riddled car, and raced toward the nearest street with the improbable, almost grotesque, speed of a madman. But he had failed to notice one of the tanks, followed by a troop of infantry, which had advanced to that very street. He was startled out of the mindless panic of his blind flight by the horrid flutter of a tank shell, winging its way past his head like some terrible bird and exploding against a building with an appalling blast. He threw himself to the ground and crawled on, crazed with fear, while more shells whistled past him like the blows of an enraged man, punching the air. Again and again the rapid flutter above his head, then the detonation, reverberating in the street as if it were a living room. The twelve meters to the street seemed a murderous eternity between life and death. He jumped up and ran, ran toward the street as if into the open arms of life, fluttering curtains, open windows, and the defaced facades of buildings accompanying him as in a dream. The seconds were monstrous waves of fear through which he struggled to make his way. He looked around and saw the barrel of the khaki monster rounding the corner like a silently threatening snout; the soldiers accompanying it, moving soundlessly, struck him as especially cruel as they occupied the nearby doorways, calling out in their nasal language for him to surrender. The next bullet whizzed past his shoulder, so close that he could feel the cold ripple of air, and struck a large store window, which shattered in bright and terrible laughter. Then he was on the ground again, crawling, twisting, changing direction like a wild animal, enveloped by the almost sweet song of the infantry's bullets and the ghastly flutter of bursting tank shells. He reached the edge of the street, sweating, filthy, and totally exhausted. The hideous khaki monster rumbled nearer as soldiers rushed from door to door. Cries and stench, noise, noise. Just as he was about to throw himself with full force against the door of a house, a shot flashed from a basement window directly across the way, grazing his arm, ricocheting off the wall, and angling into infinity with a threatening hum. He lurched in despair, near to surrender, heading up the street again, her dear, small beloved face constantly before him. Suddenly, to the right, a small side street. He threw himself into it as into an abyss, cried out, and the small face grew larger and smiled as, blind with exhaustion, almost feeling his way in spite of the bright, smiling sky, he leaned his shoulder against the first door he came to and it opened easily. He found the bolt to lock it as if he'd known the house for years, then stood silently, leaning against the door, holding his breath, listening. Scarcely a minute had passed since he had leapt from behind the bullet-riddled car to race mindlessly toward the face of his beloved.

He was pale with panic, trembling all over as if he were cold; he heard the tanks rolling closer, several of them, heard shouts from the cellars as the soldiers called back and forth in their crude, chewed-up language, he even thought he could hear the silent fall of their doom-laden rubber soles, but he seemed nailed to the spot by fear, while the street outside seemed to awaken, as if his presence alone had held it in check.

A soft cry of shock, the sort that slips out in moments of greatest danger, released him from paralysis. Startled, he turned and saw a slim, dark-haired young woman in the long, dimly lit hall, her hands stretched forward to ward him off, as delicate and unreal as a fairy tale, dressed in flowing pink.

In the blurred dusk of the hall her hands, face, and dress appeared as an almost flat surface, only the dark ink-spot of her hair stood living and solid in the gray mesh of the air. The frightened gestures relaxed, she approached slowly, and her face emerged, palpable and young, still nervous, in the light passing through the milky glass of the door. Reinhard made an urgent gesture of silence, filled with such need that she instinctively softened her steps. He listened to the sounds outside, tense and alert, as if his fate were to be wrested from that profusion of noise. His eyes searched the charming face of the young woman, and he saw in the human goodness of her gaze that she had no wish to drive him back to ruin.

He quickly surveyed the whole of her face, as if seeking confirmation, the small, delicate mouth, still drawn slightly downward by fear, the sweet, childlike forehead, the fine nose and the sturdy chin, framed and compressed into a small white plane by the raven-black hair. Then he turned his eyes aside, as if trying to see right through the milk glass, and whispered hoarsely, to her astonishment in fluent French: "If you want to help me, find me some clothes." At first she didn't seem to understand, and gazed at him in surprise, then slipped hurriedly back down the hall. He squeezed his hands together, trying to control his violent trembling as he heard them pounding at nearby doors. He worked a cigarette from his pocket with trembling hands, then started in fear at the sound of the flaring match; the silence with which the woman returned along the hall, quickly and quietly, seemed to him a precious caress. He grabbed the bundle she held out to him, walked rapidly into the darkness of the hall, and began changing as quickly as he could. It seemed an act of providence that he already had on the soft white silk shirt, for she had evidently forgotten any linen.

Now rifle butts were pounding at the door, hard and impatient, and he trembled as he remembered how weak the bolt was. But then he heard the woman's voice, and as he heard it, gentle and kind, yet so wonderfully calm and cool, he knew that he was saved; she said indignantly: "Just a moment, sir, I have to get dressed. . . ." She repeated the words in broken English, and received a coarsely muttered reply, which, although unintelligible, sounded like an obscenity delivered with a broad grin. But Reinhard had already changed, and had donned along with his clothes a wonderful, buoyant sense of freedom that intoxicated him. He felt his way toward the cellar door, threw his old stuff down the steps, and went back to the front door in his stocking feet.

The woman regarded him with a smile, and he asked her in

a whisper: "Are you really alone here?" When she nodded, he calmly pulled back the bolt on the door. A huge figure, of almost animal perfection in its proportions, a childlike, unhewn face, and the embarrassed yet still threatening question uttered in broken French: "German soldier . . . no see?" Since he had addressed his question to the woman, she answered calmly: "No," and shook her head, and, as he turned to scrutinize the man, closely and searchingly, and seemed about to seize him by the shoulder with his massive hand, she added: "This is my husband, he's—" but the word "mute" was cut off amiably by Reinhard, who pulled back the hair at his forehead with a brilliantly acted show of pride and revealed a broad, still pinkly gleaming scar that crossed his brow like the stroke of a sword: "I was wounded, comrade . . . up by the canal . . . at . . ." and he rummaged in his coat pocket as if he meant to produce his papers. "Legionnaire," he added in a murmur, but the giant, had he ever been in doubt, seemed convinced by his fluent French, and touched his cap in smiling salute and apology. There was an incomparable animal elegance in his movements as he turned and shouldered his way out the door. "That's not Europe," the woman said softly. Then the two of them were alone.

Once the peril and the compassion that provided the driving force behind this brief scene had faded, they were overcome by embarrassment. Reinhard mopped his perspiration-soaked brow and took a deep puff of his still-burning cigarette. He still believed he was half dreaming, for eternity had descended upon him, compressed into minutes. With a helpless smile he asked sadly: "What now?" It couldn't have been more than five minutes since he was standing by the car, dreaming of peace, lost in the tranquillity of the afternoon. And now he was standing helpless and destitute in this dim, cool hallway beside a woman he didn't know, astonished by her rare beauty, in misery—drowned in deepest misery. . . .

The face of the woman was cool and reserved, as if she only now realized what she had done in all the excitement. She seemed to be thinking things over as the uncanny silence of the house, heightened by the noise from the street, rippled between them, unfamiliar and oppressive.

Finally, with a gesture of resignation, she rebolted the door, stepped into the hall, and said coldly: "Come this way." There was something almost businesslike in her movements, as if she were conducting a customer into the office of a doctor or lawyer. She opened a door at the end of the hall and entered; depressed, he followed her like a condemned man.

The odor of the dim, tasteful, somewhat overdecorated room engulfed him, delicate and almost gracious, like a true expression of the woman's nature. As if peril and misery were forcing him inexorably to the rim of an abyss, he sensed with dismay that he was becoming increasingly captivated by her beauty. He closed the door softly. She sat in an armchair, her hands propped, while he stood leaning against a sideboard. "Sit down," she said, with what seemed like irritation. He sat down obediently, and as he did so, he was struck by how magnificently the trousers fit. Ridiculous, he thought. The woman's face suddenly lifted toward him like a somber disk. Her large, gray-veiled eyes were sad, and she said softly, without rancor, as if speaking to herself: "You know, I was just thinking, you may be the one who kills my husband at the front."

Reinhard shook his head wearily: "I won't kill any more people in this war, ma'am."

"Are you so sure?" she said quietly, almost imploringly. "How do you know what fate might drive you to, when you might be in a position where it's a matter of life and death to fire in some direction, and might that not be my husband? You want to make it back to Germany, don't you?"

Reinhard blushed. "I want to see my wife."

She glanced briefly at his wedding ring. "The war is far from over, and who can trust a German?" She looked at him searchingly, as if she truly wanted to sound his depths. "I should have turned you in," she continued in a flat voice. "It probably wouldn't even have cost you your life. If Robert doesn't return, I'll feel for the rest of my life that I was his murderer." She smiled suddenly, a beautiful, heartfelt smile. "I love Robert more than my life."

He felt himself turn pale. A wild, unfamiliar, tremendously powerful, seemingly irresistible desire for the woman sitting before him flooded over him, gliding like a secret sorrow. It flowed into him, and it seemed as if his own wife's beautiful face were smiling at him as well, filled with pity and love. He was so miserable, so miserable and forlorn, trapped between obstacles.

"Tell me what to do, ma'am," he said in hoarse agitation, "for all I care, you can lock me up in your cellar like an animal, or I can leave your house now and mix in with the crowd." He rose. He wanted so badly to flee, simply to flee; but then the clamor from the street rose like a tornado twisting into the heavens. Cries could be heard, doors and windows slammed.

The woman pulled open the door of the adjoining room, rushed to the window, and peered out past the curtain, breathing rapidly. Khaki figures raced down the street in retreat, and at that same moment a savage burst of fire from a German machine gun swept the roadway like a cruel, invisible broom. The fiendishly rapid spray of bullets gurgled down the canyon of the street like disaster incarnate. All the buildings seemed suddenly desolate, the facades stared emptily, gripped once more by terror. Reinhard shook his head, trembling in agitation. "They really are insane," he murmured in German, without noticing the woman's mistrustful look.

He was deeply shocked as the first gray figure rounded the corner, soiled and dusty. He knew the trooper's cynical face. It was Grote, carrying the slim black machine gun under his arm like a delicate, dangerous animal. Grote, a fine soldier constantly wavering between desertion and the possibility that he might one day wear the highest medals. Yet his face was totally miserable. Reinhard's heart beat wildly, insistently; he'd forgotten everything. He no longer realized he was wearing the soft, lightweight clothing of a civilian. The gray desolation of the army weighed once more upon his shoulders, and without looking toward the woman, he walked slowly, slowly into the hall. A dull pounding at the door awakened him from his dark, brooding mood; he took a few steps, tore open the door, and pulled a totally collapsed body in a khaki uniform inside, a split second before a new troop of gray soldiers darted around the corner and the sound of a savage whip hissed through the narrow street again.

Reinhard bent over the exhausted man, but the woman, who had followed close on his heels, grabbed his shoulder roughly and yelled: "Don't kill him!" Reinhard looked at her, releasing his hands from the fatigued man's chest, and his eyes contained equal measures of unspeakable astonishment and terrible sorrow. He gazed fixedly at her delicate, flushed face with its dark eyes and said softly, as if he could hardly trust his own words: "Do you really take me for a swine, ma'am?" Then he slowly unbuttoned the man's jacket, undid his belt, seized the inert body under the arms, and dragged him into the living room. Slowly, her arms hanging helplessly at her sides, the woman followed. He moved his hands cautiously about the man's body, sensing the silent presence of the woman at his back, pleasing and oppressive at the same time, like a gentle, inexorable wall pushing him nearer and nearer to an abyss. A pale, almost yellowish childlike face, distorted by fear, numb with exhaustion, small, fleshy hands, a shock of touchingly youthful brown hair. He could discover no wound on the body; his pulse was weak, but steady. Perhaps the youngster was only unconscious after all. Reinhard turned slowly, his gaze slipped hurriedly, nervously, past the glowing face. Her youthful, totally transfigured look of sweet shame stirred him strangely, and, his face turned toward the door, he said: "I can't find any wound." But she merely stammered: "Please forgive me. . . ." and now he had to look at her. All that was foreign and cold had fallen from her, and she was so close and familiar and so terribly beautiful that it startled him. Cheerfully, with a smile, he took the hand she offered him, pressed it firmly, so that he wouldn't feel the wild coursing of her blood, this blood a stranger to his own, and then said: "I have nothing to forgive you for, ma'am."

They both regarded this small, poor, unknown soldier as a

gift from heaven. What would have happened to them had they been left alone? Outside, in the renewed silence, the heavy tramp of boots in the street, and farther off the rattle of the machine gun. It must be at the park entrance now, near the bullet-riddled car. Reinhard washed the face of the young man while she held the bowl, then made him as comfortable as he could. He could still hear the faint beating of the boy's heart. Now they could look at each other without fear or blushing. Something akin to joy lay in their eyes, a cheerful renunciation, and they knew they needed to wage a fierce battle deep within themselves, for and against each other, to remain faithful. Once again the machine gun gnashed its teeth somewhere in the park, like a file rasping angrily across a thousand tiny, sharp fangs. Reinhard jerked as if the entire burst of gunfire had struck him in the heart. Some uncontrollable urge bound him to the terror and misery outside, and he felt he had to tear himself free, quickly and irrevocably, as from a mysterious umbilical cord. He stretched, put the washcloth aside, and said: "I'd better get rid of my uniform now. You'll be alone for a few minutes." She looked at him in surprise, slightly startled. "And what if the Ger—your countrymen capture you?" Reinhard turned toward the door. "It's not the Germans or Americans I'm running from, ma'am, it's the war. Anyway, I think the Americans are in control this evening."

It was a somber, terrible business, emptying the pockets of the miserable rags in the cellar, with their dangling, half-broken decorations, bundling them together. It seemed gruesome, like looting a corpse, and he tried to do it as quickly and hurriedly as possible, like a necessary yet still nasty task, as if he were secretly burying a murdered man. When he had placed the tangle of clothes in a trash can and concealed it beneath some rubbish, he quickly climbed the stairs again. His hands felt dirty, as if they would never be clean again, and the war, with its cruel necessities, seemed more terrible than ever.

Something akin to jealousy shot through him as he found the woman sitting beside the stranger in the living room, enveloped in the fragrance of aromatic cigarettes, but he was instantly ashamed, as if he had once again defiled himself. She had draped a blue cloak over her pale rose sundress, and he felt he would have to tie his hands to keep from taking her in his arms. He greeted the newly awakened young man with reserve. His curiously childlike and yet depraved eyes responded politely, but with the condescension of the victorious soldier facing a civilian who has remained safely in his home. *"Merci,"* he said awkwardly, offering him the pack of cigarettes with a smile, then, turning to the woman, he chewed out an unintelligible sentence in which a few words were clear: crazy . . . German . . . damned animals. Then he turned abruptly to Reinhard and asked in broken French: "What are they still fighting for, these Germans?" He gestured vaguely outside, where the machine gun again raised its hoarse, threatening bark. Reinhard looked from one to the other uncertainly, but the woman calmed him with a slight shake of her head. This quiet, gentle indication of a bond moved him so deeply that a shiver ran through him.

The whole house was suddenly shaken by a powerful detonation. This was followed by waves of weapon fire in the area. The woman sprang up and leaned against the wall, pale and trembling. Reinhard approached her, placed his hand on her arm, and said calmly: "You're safe, ma'am, that's artillery fire.

No, no, believe me, you have nothing to worry about." He watched the stranger's face closely, but a smile triumphed over the young man's initial shock as he cried: "Those are our shells . . . those are ours!"

Several more shells exploded among the buildings with deafening noise, the dark murmur of advancing tanks could be heard, and the abrupt crack of their cannons, sounding like a sudden blowout, followed by the shattering din of the impact. A few minutes later, from behind the curtain, they again saw the gray figures of the Germans running down the street, a frightening indifference in their gait.

The tanks rolled past the corner again, heading up the street, as the small stranger with the pale child's face smiled, laid a bar of chocolate on the table, shook hands warmly with them both, and left the building. The silence of the house enveloped them again, and now they were alone.

Reinhard went to the door, which the young man had left open, and stuck his head out for an instant before bolting it, feeling the cool, gentle evening air, with its delicate summery smells already offering a foretaste of autumn as it descended upon the beautiful, incomparable city. And perhaps it was the greatest offense of his life, the greatest, that he didn't simply leave the house, but instead turned back, slowly and heavily, into the dusk of the hall, which had become thicker and darker.

The woman stood at the open window, her arms crossed, staring out into the evening at the gardens. Like a piece of bad theater, the sound of voices, high-pitched and somehow tinged with excited joy, arose once more from the street, and it seemed as if these scenes might alternate throughout eternity.

As if wishing to hide even from herself, the woman stood in

the recess of the window and did not turn as Reinhard entered. She gazed into the evening sky, its blue now touched with gentle shades of rose and lilac, stretching like a delicate tent above the splendid summer day now coming to a close, a day on which so many men had perished in the cruel arms of war. She seemed to shiver, although the soft breeze was still mild and pleasant. Her shoulders were hunched, she had buttoned the fine blue wool cloak about her, and her pale face, with the small red fruit of the mouth, appeared almost dead. The room was already wrapped in darkness, although it was still bright outside, as bright and friendly and beautiful as Paris, the incomparable city in which the war still raged. Reinhard gazed at her spellbound. Just half a second more, he thought, I'll just look at her, just look, then I'll slip away as quickly and quietly as I can. I'll run and run until the nearness of the distant woman I love extinguishes the terrible, consuming fire within me.

But the woman turned around, suddenly, abruptly, as if she had just awakened, and said softly: "You'll have to leave the house by way of those gardens when it's completely dark. Believe me, a thousand pairs of eyes have seen you enter the house, and any one of them would recognize you again. They don't think you're here anymore, because the house has already been searched."

He protested in a state of shock: "But that means I'll have to wait here several more hours." He felt fear rise within him, wild desires and opposing thoughts, and he was surprised by the joyful smile with which she said: "Do you find it so terrible to be my prisoner until darkness falls?" adding with a wry smile: "But wait a moment . . ." She walked past him and he heard her leave the house.

He breathed a sigh of relief. Was he so weak and foolish he couldn't spend two hours beside this beautiful woman without succumbing ineluctably to the terrible sin of betrayal? He had carried the image of his beloved unscathed through all the dangers and temptations, the infinite agonies of war. Was he to give it up now, without wishing to, seduced by the dark, melodious voice of ruin hovering over this city, trapped now in the dusk of this house? Yes, it would be truly stupid to risk his escape for a foolish weakness. Smiling, he lit one of the American's cigarettes and turned on the light. But it seemed as if the dusk, the sweet sense of being lost, couldn't be banished by the warm, bright flood of light, either. It hovered among furniture, in the gaps, even above the reddish lamp shade itself, the sweet fragrance of being lost, drawing him into its spell. Ghastly and sweet, it flowed in, as if the joyful visage of the beautiful city was dissolving into insane caresses, blurred and enticing, as if enveloped by the mists of ruin.

The noise of battle spread steadily throughout the city. From time to time it fell silent, only to burst forth again like the dull blasts of a trumpet. The war's progress could be measured easily by its sounds; it was actually possible to sense the increasing depth and expanse of the blows, to feel the gray soldiers' weakening resistance, and in the streets, as the curtain lifted, the sounds of life swelled forth again.

The evening slowly filled the last bright light of day with blue shadows. It seemed to fall softly, tenderly, friendly and familiar, no more than the darker sister of the cheerful day. Twilight seemed to smile upon this immense and beautiful city, to drape its vast, dark blue cloak around her, as if it couldn't be angry with her, enfolding her in a quiet, loving, and ineffably tender embrace, openly, with no thought for the poor hearts of those who stand aside in misery, weeping, weeping in the arms of longing.

Reinhard turned the light back off. For an instant it seemed completely dark, but then the last gleams of daylight plunged through the open window into the thick dusk of the room. The window was like a benevolent shaft in a prison. Delicate reddish gleams flowed in; they seemed mingled inextricably with the confusing, yet bittersweet smells of the evening, breath and light in one, which wafted beneath the gentle trees of the boulevard. They penetrated to the young man hidden behind the curtains and breathing deeply, brushing him like the terrible caress of a beautiful woman who teases but will not yield. He groaned as if his life's blood were streaming forth, and felt his misery, his total abandonment in this foreign, hostile city, like a single, massive wound, lashed by the inescapable blandishment of his senses. He tore himself away as if he had been anchored to this shadowy play, stumbled through the dusk to the door, pulled it open, and hurried down the hall to the front entrance. But then he paused as if nailed to the spot, for he heard fate itself approaching. The front door opened and the soft steps of the woman came toward him. He saw nothing, nothing at all in the darkness of the hall, as if it were a solid fabric, but never, never in the thousands of seconds that long afternoon had he seen more clearly. He saw her whole, his heart was torn from him, and as the tiny steps approached, he braced himself against the wall, as if forced backwards by an invisible power. His eyes closed, his entire being writhed in pain, and he simply reached out, vaguely, as if he were trying to catch a bird flying past, and at the first tender touch he sensed that she too was unable to flee. And as her tears burned upon his cheeks, he longed for the entire darkness of night to crash down around them and bury them in its rubble.

When they awakened, they were so distant ice water might have been flowing between them, distant and cold, lying together a bad dream, while the milky light of the moon streamed mockingly through the open window of the room. She turned her face aside with a shudder and her entire being, mysterious and unfathomable, seemed hidden with her face behind the dark curtain of her hair. Reinhard rose, passed his hand wearily through his hair. He was shivering. Provocative and threatening, the uncanny stillness entered the haze woven of their own confusion within the room, where despairing caresses seemed to have taken hold like poisons.

He slowly pulled on his shoes, which stood beneath the wardrobe as if awaiting him. He shuddered, shuddered again, and a wild fear kept him from turning around; never had he suffered such misery as in this cold night hour, which seemed to mock the tenderness of day and evening, the hour in which, in this deeply foreign city, the myriad dangers of a daring flight ahead, he creeps from the bedroom of a beautiful woman whose sobs express the desolation lodged in his own miserable heart, arid and ineradicable. No, never again in his life could he turn back.

He moved slowly, cautiously, as if fearing to awaken the stillness, to the window; but as he was about to swing over the low sill, the muffled sound of her bare feet froze him in his tracks. He felt the blood flow like ice through his veins and, trembling as if he were about to look directly into the true, naked face of death, he quickly turned his head. And it was strange that this lovely face, sweeter and more beautiful than ever, with its small, smiling bud of a mouth, that this face, like a gently compelling mirror, forced from him a joyful, open, and innocent smile. There was no longer the slightest fiber of his being that this woman desired. Her eyes simply compelled him to throw off the entire burden, and with her small, slender hand, she passed him a slim bundle of banknotes, which he stuck in his pocket without looking. He seized her hand unhesitatingly and pressed it. "This may help you," she said in a small voice, "and don't be sad. The three who love us: God, your wife, and my husband, may well forgive us," and she kissed him quickly and lightly on the forehead. Then he swung himself out and walked toward the cold face of the moon.

The Mad Dog

THE SERGEANT PUSHED OPEN THE door and said: "Take a look at him. Is he . . . ?" He left his cigarette in his mouth. I approached the motionless figure lying on a bier. Someone perched on a stool beyond the bier rose quickly and said: "Good evening." I recognized the chaplain and nodded. He installed himself at the head of the body.

I turned irritably to the policeman and glanced at his burning cigarette: "Could I have a little more light, please? I can't see a thing." He mounted a chair and arranged the hanging lamp with a cord so that its glow fell directly on the stiffened body. Now that I could see the corpse in full light, I drew back involuntarily. I've seen plenty of dead men, but every time I see one I'm disturbed by the realization that I'm looking at a human being, a person who lived, and suffered, and loved.

I saw at once that he was dead. Not by any medical indication; I sensed it and knew it. But I had been summoned to certify his death officially, so I got down to business. It was my legal duty, after all, to go through the well-rehearsed motions with which human science gropes toward mysteries. The recumbent figure looked ghastly.

His reddish hair was soaked and matted with blood and dirt, practically glued to his head. I made out a few wounds inflicted by blows and cuts. A terrible laceration scored his face, as if a rasp had been pulled across it. His mouth was twisted, the small pale nose flattened; his hands cramped at his sides, still clenched in death; the clothes filthy and smeared with blood. You could sense the infernal rage with which he had been hit, kicked, and gashed; he had been killed with bestial pleasure. I took hold of his jacket resolutely and undid the few buttons that had not been ripped away. Oddly enough his skin was white and tender as a child's; no blood or dirt had penetrated the cloth.

The policeman suddenly bent over me, so near that I could feel his heavy breath, and with a glance at the body, said indifferently: "The party's over, huh?" I stared at him for a few seconds, feeling my face twitch with rage, almost with hate.

My eyes must have said enough. He removed the sweetly stinking cigarette from his mouth with a disconcerted air, then slipped away. At the doorway he added: "Just let me know, Doc." I felt freed somehow. Now I began my examination in earnest. How ridiculous to place a stethoscope upon this chest, to feel this pulse, to carry out the whole helpless charade upon this miserable, flayed body. He couldn't have died from the wounds to his head. Should I take the easy way out medical science offers these days and write on the death certificate: *circulatory failure . . . exhaustion . . . malnourishment*? I don't know if I laughed. I could discover nothing but the head wounds, which must have been terribly painful, but could scarcely have been fatal, having barely penetrated the outer structure of the skull. They must have been inflicted in blind rage.

Even in this desolate state his uncannily narrow, white face resembled a knife. He must have been a cold, daring fellow, I thought. I slowly rebuttoned his jacket, instinctively brushing the strands of bloody, dirty hair back from his forehead. It seemed as if he were smiling scornfully, mockingly. Then I looked at the chaplain, who had been standing at my side, pallid and silent, a quiet man I knew well. "Murdered?" I asked softly. He simply nodded, then replied in an even softer voice than mine: "A murderer, murdered." I gave a start, then stared once more at the knife-sharp, pale face, which seemed to be laughing, even beneath the agonizing wounds and abuse, cold and arrogant. Horror constricted my throat; it was horrible, this corpse in the gloomy room, drenched by the brutal lamp's harsh circle of light, while everything else lay in darkness. The bare bier . . . a few old stools . . . the walls with their crumbling plaster . . . and this dead body in a tattered gray uniform.

I looked at the chaplain almost imploringly. I was dizzy with exhaustion, fear, and nausea. The policeman's cigarette had finished me off. I had been going all afternoon on an empty stomach, entering miserable dens, powerless, helpless, absurdly at the mercy of circumstances. Although I had seen many things that day, a murdered murderer was still a rarity, even in this city.

"A murderer?" I asked, lost in thought. The chaplain pushed his stool toward me: "Sit down, please," and after I had automatically obeyed him, he continued, leaning on the plank-bed: "You don't know him then? You really don't?" He looked at me as if he almost doubted that I had my wits about me. "No," I said wearily, "I don't know him." The chaplain shook his head: "You get around so much, I thought you would have heard of the Mad Dog." I jumped up in shock . . . my God! "The Mad Dog, here—that face!" I stood beside the chaplain, both of us staring at the pallid, disfigured corpse.

"Did he have time to receive the sacraments?" I asked softly. I waited some time for his response. The chaplain didn't appear to have heard me, and I didn't want to ask again. The silence was nearly stifling, and when the chaplain answered, it seemed as if several minutes had passed: "No . . . but he could have. I was with him almost an hour. He was tremendously agitated and alert, before he"—he looked at me—"passed away."

The chaplain stretched his hands out helplessly toward the corpse, as if he wished to caress him. His poor, narrow child's face appeared rigid with emotion—I can think of no other way to put it. He pushed his blond hair back as if in despair, and then blurted in agitation: "You . . . you may think I'm crazy, but I'd like to stay with him a while, until they come to get him, yes, I don't want to leave him alone. He truly loved only one person in his life, and that person betrayed him; you can laugh if you want, but . . . aren't we all guilty? And if I stay with him for a while . . . perhaps . . ." He looked at me with a vague, troubled obstinacy in his eyes. They were blue, with dark circles of hunger clinging beneath them, almost like stigmata. No, the word *crazy* never crossed my mind. And laugh at him, my God! "I'll stay with you," I said.

We were silent for the time it takes to say an Our Father and a Hail Mary. Harsh, strident laughter spilled into our silence from the guard room, women's voices, shrill shrieks. I returned slowly and released the lamp so that it dangled in its former position. The entire room was evenly enveloped in a dull, flat light; the ghastly corpse looked gentler, less rigid, almost more lifelike. Nothing is more merciless than this light, this electric light so appropriate to their cigarettes, their cadaverous faces, their weary lewdness. I hate that electric light.

The laughter from the guard room swelled and receded.

The chaplain started, as if brushed by a private fear, as if some terrible memory had touched him. "Sit down, Doctor," he said quietly. "I want to tell you something about him."

I sat down as asked, while the chaplain sat sideways on the plank-bed. We turned our backs to the dead man.

"By strange coincidence," the chaplain began, "he and I were born in the same year, nineteen twenty-eight. He told me everything; you know, I'm not sure whether he was talking to me, or himself, or someone who wasn't here. He stared at the ceiling as he spoke, talking feverishly, in fact he probably had a fever. He never knew his parents, you know, never went to school. He was dragged around various places. His first memories, sometime between the war and the inflation, were of the police dragging off the man he thought of up to then as his father, a crude, cowardly fellow, half tramp, half thief, and half laborer, from some block of flats or other on the outskirts of town.

"Picture a squalid room in which a poor, chronically abused woman lives with a perpetually drunken, lazy, and cowardly brute . . . that's the whole of it. You know the situation, Doctor. Once his alleged father was sent off to prison for several years his life settled down somewhat. His aunt—he found out later that this eternally irritable, hateful woman was his aunt—got a job at a factory. The police saw that he was sent to school. And there he stood out because of his unusual intelligence. Can you picture it, Doctor"—the chaplain looked at me—"that knife-sharp face slicing through dull classes at school? Well, he became the top student, but what does that say when in fact he towered so far above the others? And he was ambitious. The teachers recommended that he attend the gymnasium; the minister took an interest in the matter, but this woman, his aunt, opposed the idea angrily; it made her furious. She acted as if they wanted to murder him; she did everything she could to restrict him to her own miserable, crude surroundings. She made all sorts of difficulties, you see, insisting on her rights as his guardian; she harassed him whenever he was home . . . he wasn't to try to 'rise' in the world. But she was evidently no match for the combined powers of his teachers and the priest. He was awarded a scholarship to a boarding school, was taken on as a full-time student, and soon exceeded their highest expectations. Everything came easily to him. He learned Latin and Greek as well as mathematics and German . . . and he was religious. Yet he wasn't one of those humble types who accepts everything and quietly grinds away at their studies. He was creative, clever, his knowledge in religious instruction was almost that of a theologian. In short, he was a real star. And not once did he recall the milieu he had escaped with anything but horror and disgust; he felt no compassion for it, he shuddered at the thought of it. He even stayed at school during vacations, making himself useful in the library, in the office. There was no doubt that he would follow in the footsteps of his patrons. But he was willful and arrogant, with stubborn self-confidence. 'I think deep down I always felt contempt for all of them, without realizing it,' he said to me. Grinding his teeth in rage, he took whatever punishments his pride occasioned, but was seldom disciplined. He was a star, putting them all to shame. They overlooked things now and then; only when he went too far, or neglected to show the expected humility, was he punished.

"But the older he grew, the more the world tempted him. Riches, fame, power: His heart would speed up when he thought of them; and by the time he was sixteen he had already inwardly abandoned the idea of staying in the order, although he said nothing about it, since he wanted to complete his studies. All genuine religious feeling dissolved in the constant tension caused by this new attitude. The world was so tempting, you see, the whole false blossoming of politics back then, like a communal lust for chaos, the fearful life of unburied corpses; it tempted him. On the other hand, he didn't want to lose his chance to finish school; the misery, the old, terrible domestic misery was still strongly engraved in his memory. He didn't exactly play the hypocrite, but he became calculating. Quite imperceptibly, calculation poisoned him over the months and years. He almost went bad; at any rate he lost what little faith he had.

"When he completed his degree and coldly informed the fathers of his decision, the whole situation was of course somewhat embarrassing, but he turned his back on them without a hint of shame; he 'simply burnt his bridges.' He had his diploma, not a word had been said linking his free education to his entry into the order. He severed all connections with the school and went out into the world, armed only with an excellent education and fierce ambition. He didn't have one decent suit, not a penny to his name, nothing.

"But then one of his schoolmates, a certain Becker, turned out to be a real friend. Becker, whose parents were rich, was studying theology. He supported him financially, talking his parents out of some of the money and providing the rest from his own savings. So Herold left the school. . . . By the way, did you know that he was named Theodor Herold?" The chaplain looked at me inquiringly. How would I know his name? I shook my head.

The noise from the guard room kept threatening to drown us out. Noise . . . shouts . . . the senseless bellowing of those who voluntarily allow themselves to be incarcerated in the prison of a uniform. The chaplain fell silent, then seemed almost to choke on his words as he said: "What good does it do to tell you all this? We should be praying instead; it's just about the only thing one can do, don't you think?" He gave me a tormented look, as if he were about to collapse beneath an invisible weight. Then he folded his hands. I took him gently by the arm, and I don't know if it was curiosity that impelled me to say: "Go on with your story, please. I want to know everything."

The chaplain looked uneasily at me; he almost seemed mentally disturbed. He stared at me blankly, as if he didn't recognize me, and seemed to be searching his memory to recall who I was; then he took his head in his hands. "Oh, yes," he said in a despairing voice, "Pardon me . . . I . . . I," he gestured helplessly. And then he continued:

"It appears that Becker truly wanted to help Herold. They were studying at a university, and although Becker was somewhat restricted by living in a church hostel, he visited him often, talked with him, and no doubt tried to reawaken his buried religious impulse. But his support was in no way dependent upon this. They argued at times, that's clear, discussing things all young men not yet dead discuss: religion and the concept of the *Volk* and so on, but remained friends through it all. And, although he never said so, he respected Becker, the only person he didn't despise. He loved Becker; and not simply because he supported him, but for the unconditional manner in which he gave the money. Well, no doubt you have some idea of the relationship. Becker must have been an ardent young man who still believed in grace. For the first few semesters all the theology students still believed in grace, which was later often unconsciously replaced by belief in the vicar-general.

"Herold was just as great a phenomenon of intelligence and wit at the university as he had been in school. He not only despised his frivolous and less able fellow students, but his professors too, none of whom, as he put it, could be considered 'a true spiritual guide.' In the meantime he prepared for a possible career in politics. You can imagine how quickly the party absorbed such an intelligent young man.

"But then something terrible happened: He became a soldier, and there was no antidote for that. He hated the military beyond anything he'd known, hated it deeply, for when he tried to make a career there, a strange thing happened: That same officer caste which had welcomed dim-witted criminals from the dankest swamps of society insisted that new recruits meet certain social standards: and of course he failed to meet the conditions of this hierarchy of ignorance. His hatred now firmly established, he made his first declaration of war against society. He saw through the absolute political cowardice of these yes-men. He glowed with white-hot rage and scorn, but of course got nowhere against the well-established clique, and the dull and dreary life in the barracks seemed even more terrible than the misery of his childhood years. War seemed to offer him salvation, and he volunteered for one of those units which, steeped in that spirit which denies all true values, considered the murder conducted behind the lines, known as the destruction of racially inferior types, equivalent to the murder at the front, called war." The chaplain paused in misery and covered his face with his hands, breathing heavily. "Imagine that razor-sharp face among those troops, filled with hate, in that social order which became blinder and more cold-blooded with every passing year under the terrible pressures of war, yoked to the triumphal car of a criminal who denied all values—that gloomy triumphal car whose rotten wheels were soon to crumble, and which collapsed at last in a flood of stinking gasoline fumes.

"Repelled at first by his associates in spite of having volunteered, then increasingly entangled in emotions that bind a bloodthirsty mob, Herold still kept in touch with Becker, who wrote to him, warned him, admonished him. Herold even visited him on leave, congratulating him on his ordination as a priest. Even afterwards he maintained contact with Becker, whom he truly loved, a word he never used, given his unusual shyness. He sent Becker packages with items that were scarce back home: cigars, soap, lard, and so on. He wrote letters, sent small packets, but revealed nothing of his spiritual condition. No more discussions on religion and worldviews. He felt irrevocably bound to the gang he had stumbled into, often filled with bitter regret, horrified by the streams of blood mingled with dirt, terrified by bestial cruelties, all these emotions jumbled together with unexamined notions of race, honor, and unconditional obedience, the Fatherland, the master race. He became an officer in those units, was wounded several times, distinguished himself, was decorated. But none of that could expunge the uneasy feeling of guilt. He seemed deeply troubled.

"And in the chaos of anxiety, hatred, and remorse, the worst for him was that Becker ceased writing. He heard nothing from him for over a year. He attributed his silence to the breakdown of communications, the total confusion of an 'incomparable system.' Although he blamed it on these external factors the dark suspicion remained that Becker no longer cared about him. And the closer the end came, the inevitable, disastrous end, the more defiled he felt, burdened with indescribable acts of cruelty.

"Only the thought of Becker, who might perhaps help him, sustained him. A series of clever maneuvers allowed him to avoid capture by the Russians. He managed to smuggle himself through the Russian front lines as a Russian soldier until he reached the area controlled by the Western powers. Here he disappeared, well furnished with money and provisions, somewhere in his devastated hometown, in one of the thousands of hiding places no one would ever discover; and here too he avoided capture. Then he began a careful search for Becker. For him, Becker symbolized salvation. He had no clear idea what sort of help he expected; he was totally broken. The dark water of fear, disgust, and guilt had risen to his chin; he simply wanted to speak with someone who wouldn't threaten him, wouldn't reject him. He saw Becker as the representative of a religion which, contrary to all secular custom, did not judge, did not condemn—the religion that he himself had loved as a child and young boy, whose reflected splendor still shone upon him, without his knowledge.

"Disguised as a disabled soldier, he limped out of his hiding place and began, amid the hopeless chaos, to search for Becker, whom he knew had been a chaplain in a small town. He finally managed to reach the town by hitching a ride in an American military truck. He found the village undamaged, its inhabitants still frightened and confused. And he found Becker. His heart pounding with happiness, he entered the rectory.

"Becker was cold and indifferent. He had broken off the correspondence intentionally. Their entire friendship had died, and Becker acted strangely, treating him as if he'd met him once years ago and had simply run into him again, just another former acquaintance. Herold was shocked by the cool reserve with which his only friend received him, but the dark tumult of torment, blood, and guilt which had gathered within him was too powerful to restrain. He opened his heart to Becker, telling him everything, every single thing, things he could never have written. And when he had finished, and he had nothing more to say or ask, he stared helplessly at Becker. He told me that for the first time in his life, he found himself totally defenseless.

"Becker said nothing. He appeared touched in his professional role as a spiritual adviser, as a paid official of the state, but in human terms, Becker had been completely deadened by everything he had seen, heard, and experienced; by the horrors of the retreat, by hunger, confusion, fear, and bombs. Becker only had a few phrases to offer, you know the sort—ready-made clichés from the spiritual five-and-dime store, the stuff handed out in some confessionals after absolution, one to a customer and on your way . . . next, please! Of course he urged him to go to confession, to pray, to become a better man . . . imagine!"

The chaplain seized me firmly by the shoulder and forced my weary face in his direction. His eyes flared excitedly, like sparkling blue lights, his poor, pale face was flushed, his mouth twitching. We faced each other almost like combatants, here by the bier bearing the corpse of the Mad Dog! But I was so tired, so very tired. And yet deep, deep within me lay an urgent, passionate interest in this human destiny, and I had to hear how it had ended.

"You see," the chaplain groaned, "I can easily imagine it, because I've done it so many times myself. I can picture it in living detail. Becker no longer had a personal relationship with him. In the face of this terrible torment he produced nothing but a cool, professional response. Perhaps he was worn down, dulled, as may happen to priests in the confessional. . . . My God, nothing but adultery and baseness, year after year! Perhaps, as a doctor, you understand. You find a corpse less gruesome than thousands of others do who've seen far fewer corpses and far less blood, in spite of the war. Unburied bodies are less disturbing and less moving to priests than they are to those who have never peered into the hearts of so-called decent human beings. My God . . . that's how it must have been for Becker, you see. The demonic frenzy of the final months of the war had died away and we were in the doldrums, the wind had fallen and everything was still, a becalmed void. Becker was cool toward him. Indifferent, perhaps even dismissive. Herold said: 'He pushed me back into my personal abyss. . . .' And then he plunged into a totally destructive rage.

"He must have been denounced by people who noticed him and found him suspicious. The police were after him; he had to change hiding places several times. They hounded him through the piles of rubble. In the midst of a broad expanse of ruins in the inner city, he finally discovered a bombed-out building with an undamaged cellar, easily accessible and difficult to find, and here, motivated by burning hate, he brooded a few days before emerging as the 'Mad Dog.' He found accomplices easily enough—he couldn't bear to be alone, although he was arrogant and domineering with his henchmen. First they stole enough to make themselves comfortable. Then—planning in cold blood—they amassed a large supply of stolen goods on the black market, stocked their rooms with provisions, and began a hideous game. The whole plan was his; he was the acknowledged leader and judge. He turned up, with a certain aura of mystery, when his henchmen had carried out the burglary and prepared the victim or victims. He declared the method of death according to his mood . . . shooting . . . stabbing or hanging . . . and often simply terrorized them, leaving them quaking under the constant threat." The chaplain paused for a moment. "They killed twenty-three people that way . . . twenty-three."

The two of us stared at the motionless body, moved by a deep feeling of horror—cold terror in our veins. The murderer's pale red hair shimmered softly through patches of blood and dirt in the dismal light of the room. The cold, thin-lipped mouth seemed still to be smiling, scornful and cruel, appearing to mock our words, our entire conversation. I turned, trembling, and waited uneasily for the chaplain to turn toward me as well. I felt menaced by doleful spirits, and thought his poor, humane face might offer some consolation. But the chaplain remained silent a long time, staring at the dead man . . . a long time. I don't know if he startled me out of my thoughts, or prayers, or merely from a state lost in fear, when he touched me lightly on the shoulder. Now his voice was gentle, almost consoling: "And strangest of all, this man, who was never close to any woman, who lived a life of almost celibate purity, died because of a woman. And it occurred to me he might still be alive, might have been a more humane person, had he found a woman to love, or succumbed only to those vices of all weak men—alcohol and tobacco. In some mysterious sense, he remained chaste. No ruined fragment from paradise could deceive him. And his downfall was brought about by a woman, added to the gang against his will, who wormed her way in, in spite of his objections, his furious outbursts, a woman he could never control, although she committed several murders under his leadership. Worst of all, she was in love with him, and was driven by months of scorn and rejection to murder him. She incited the others, and they fell upon him with a fury more terrible than that reserved for other victims, for it is a diabolical, profoundly shocking enigma that down deep, Hell hates nothing quite so much as itself. They practically tore him to pieces. Yet he was still alive when they found him here at the door with a slip of paper in his breast pocket, on which was written, in a literate hand: *The Mad Dog, for burial by the police.* It was a woman's writing. . . ."

I no longer had the strength to move. Lost, I stared at the dirty ceiling. My God, was I hungry, tired? I was miserable, the absolute horror of it all beyond my grasp, immersed in my own total wretchedness, incapable of prayer. I felt buried beneath the rubble of despair of our entire world by the chaplain's report, and a dull, dark personal fear held me in its rigid, iron claws. Then, as if the words were already dashed to pieces within my mouth, I managed to ask: "Do you think that he . . . ?"

But the chaplain had turned around once more. He seemed to be praying, and—strangely—I too was forced to turn and view the body, the unchanged corpse, smeared with blood and filth. Perhaps I prayed, I don't know. . . . My entire being was a blend of fear and torment and dull foreboding.

But who can describe this state of dull, defensive listlessness in which the mind retains a sharp clarity, a coldness possible only in thought?

Then the door was yanked open so noisily it sounded as if the building was about to be brought down around our heads, and as we turned around, shocked and startled, a harsh voice called out: "All right, let's get the body and—" But then three uniformed figures noticed us and approached more quietly. Things seemed so strangely bright upon their entrance. One of them, a slim, dark-haired man with an impassive face, said quietly: "Good evening," and turned to the other two: "All right now . . ." But the chaplain, who'd watched in shock all the while, as if lost in thought, finally came to himself. He raised his hands to ward them off and cried out: "No . . . no . . . let me do that. . . ." He quickly turned and gathered the frayed human bundle fearlessly, ignoring the shocked cry: "But Father!"

He looked as if he were carrying a dead lover with despairing tenderness.

I followed as in a dream through the warm, terrible brightness of the guard room, out into the damp, dark street, covered with wet patches of dirty snow. A car waited outside, its motor growling, coughing. Slowly, tenderly, the chaplain placed the body on a sack of straw inside the vehicle. There was a smell of gasoline and oil, of war and terror. The darkness, the merciless darkness of winter, lay across the empty facades of the buildings like an unbearable burden.

"But . . . no . . . you can't do that. . . ." one of the policemen cried as the chaplain got into the car. But the third made an unambiguous circular motion at his temple—while the dark-haired one stood by quietly, with what seemed to me a pained smile.

The chaplain gestured for me to come closer, and in spite of the swelling roar of the engine, I heard the words he whispered softly to me, as if it were a secret: "He cried in the end, you know. . . . I wiped away the tears before you came . . . because the tears—" But the car suddenly pulled away with a powerful surge, and I saw only a final helpless gesture of the figure in black as he was carried off into the cold, gloomy canyons of the destroyed city.

The Rendezvous

I WENT TO THE QUAY early to meet her. It had been pouring rain for days. The ground of the promenade had softened, and leaves were rotting in the puddles. Although it was mid-August, the smell of autumn was already in the trees, the café terraces had been cleared, the white chairs and tables stacked and hastily covered with canvas. Nearly all the guests had departed; not a person was in sight. A thick, humid haze floated above the water, almost obscuring the strands of rain. The only other person in view was an employee of the shipping company whose cap was visible behind the small window of his tiny ticket booth.

The waiters stood shivering in the corners of the hotel lobbies, waiting on the few guests seeking afternoon coffee or tea.

A week ago I'd sat down beside her in the cinema. I had arrived early, far too early, and as I walked past the yawning usher into the empty, brightly lit movie house, the first thing I saw was the glare of the projector, its flickering light casting black threads upon the bright rectangle of the screen, gently shifting, tumbling about in the void; and right at the front of the empty hall, near the screen, I saw her, just her delicate neck and green raincoat, and although I had a ticket for one of the better seats, I walked forward and sat down beside her.

I felt the damp rising slowly around me now, leaching itself coolly to me, but I didn't care. My gaze was fixed on the bend in the Rhine where the boat would appear at any moment. The blackboard on which the arrival time had been written in chalk bore only a few smeared, grayish white lines, and water was dripping from the clapper of the bell used to announce arrivals and departures, faster and faster, like a leaky faucet.

A black barge appeared at the far end of the bend, being towed wearily, irritatingly slowly, upstream. I looked at my watch: It was a few minutes to five. If the boat intended to depart again on schedule, ten minutes from now, it had to round the bend at any moment. The man behind the little window of the booth was enjoying a cigarette, his red face veiled now and then by smoke. My coat was already dark from the rain.

The barge had not yet cleared the bend, towing its rear section like a wounded reptile dragging its tail. Just then the fellow opened the booth and his deep voice called out to me: "Pretty boring, isn't it, Doctor?"

I recognized him now. His wife ran a tobacco store somewhere back up the quay, and not an hour ago I'd bought tobacco there and had a long chat with him about the pros and cons of various brands.

"Just recognized you," he said, glancing at my cap. "Come on in for a bit."

He squeezed up against the side of the booth facing the promenade and gestured that I was welcome to take the other side. We stood together like two guards in a sentry box.

"Lousy weather," he resumed, "bloody lousy. Whole season's ruined."

"Yep," I said, and stared out again at the bend in the river. Then I exclaimed, "There!" as a white boat, lighter and faster, pulled alongside and passed the black barge.

"Waiting for someone? Your wife?"

"Yes," I said, and instantly regretted having joined him. It would have been more pleasant to stand in the rain and know that in a quarter of an hour I would be sitting at a table with her, drinking hot tea. The man was so close to me that his curious eyes almost touched my forehead.

I kept my eyes glued on the prow of the white boat, which was now passing under the bridge, still in midstream. It was difficult to see the banks, which were veiled by the vapor of the rain, and the lofty, gloomy mountains floated ghostlike above the haze.

"Ah, love . . ." the old man said, and shoved his cap back on his head. Staring at the boat, I followed its every move as if I myself were on the river, clasping my hands tightly as I recalled how I had simply reached out in the dark, as the film began. I took her hand and held it, the hand of a stranger who pulled back at first, then gave in, a small hand, hot with shame. Now and then, when the dull shimmer of light from the screen fell upon us, we would glance at one another: I saw a narrow face with pale, serious eyes that seemed to be asking something, and later, when the film had ended, she tried to flee, to lose herself in the crowd, but I spotted her green raincoat again at the tram station.

The boat was now making its way toward the bank from midriver, and only when the man from the booth left and hurried down the smooth gangway did I realize how close the boat was. The motor was clearly audible, and people in raincoats were visible standing by the front exit. The bell was already clanging, its tones ringing out in the rain clouds like signals at sea. I stepped outside, and only then, at that moment, did I realize I felt no touch of joy; only anxiety, restlessness, and the prickling sense of danger that tempts a driver to floor the accelerator on a series of sharp curves.

I tossed my cigarette into a puddle and walked down the gangway. The old man, standing at the bottom, dropped a thick pad between the boat and the piling. A rope was slung over the side of the boat, and the old man wrapped it around an iron stanchion. Then the deckhand slid the gangplank across. I stared blankly at the entrance. Not even her green cape could free me entirely from my trance. . . .

"Good day, Frau Doctor," said the old man, who was now unloading and stacking cases of empty soft-drink bottles.

I took her arm without looking at her and drew her along with me. "Thank you," I said hoarsely.

She sighed deeply, but said nothing.

I squeezed her arm mutely. The bell rang out again behind us, and the motor swelled, then receded as we walked through the puddles on the promenade and entered the hotel.

The lobby was nearly empty. I removed her cape and saw for the first time that she was carrying a small suitcase. "Sorry," I said softly, and took the case, hanging up her cape and freeing myself from my own damp coat and cap. The old art dealer's widow who had forced her company upon me that morning, drinking brandy and regaling me with cynical anecdotes, was sitting in the lobby. She glanced up at us, then returned to her pastry. The only other person present was an old gentleman who had besieged the newsstand by noon.

"What would you like to drink?" I asked.

"Tea, or something hot." She didn't turn around, and I was offered only the delicate fragrance of her perfume, mingled with the fine haze produced by the rain. I sat down opposite her and called for the waiter, who had been lounging in the corner, keeping an eye on us.

I gave him our order.

We smoked in silence. From time to time we glanced at each other, but whenever our eyes met we would look away. In the stillness we heard only the gentle murmur of the rain, a faint clinking from the table of the art dealer's widow, who was devoting herself wholeheartedly to her torte, and a low conversation between the barmaid and two waiters, which largely drowned itself in the thick carpets and curtains.

I felt my jaw twitch nervously; it was a relief when the waiter arrived. Even the aroma of the strong tea helped. Our hands touched over the sugar bowl; I took her hand firmly and squeezed it, but she pulled away, turning pale, staring in shock at my hand. I followed her startled gaze, and my own hand, with its thick pale fingers, seemed strange to me, strange and uncanny, as if I'd never seen it before. I had forgotten to remove my wedding ring.

"For heaven's sake," I said softly, "aren't you glad to be here?"

"No," she said, shaking her head firmly.

I stirred my tea.

"Are you?" she asked.

I said nothing.

Her skin was white and shining, so cool, and her dark hair gleamed with moisture.

"Did you have a nice trip?"

"Yes," she said quietly, "it was a nice trip, splendid really. On the water like that, properly fogged in, and it smelled so nice. The only bad thing was having to stop here. I would have loved to go on, on up the Rhine in that rain to . . . yes, to Basel for all I care. Let me go," she said suddenly. I looked at her: She was pale and her lips were trembling.

"That's crazy," I said quietly, "why did you come, then?"

"Let me go."

"You probably came just to drive me crazy. Waiter!" I called out loudly.

"Let me go."

The waiter came strolling in from the lobby. "Yes?" he asked.

"Take my wife's suitcase to my room, please."

"Yes, sir."

"Let me go," she said, when the waiter had disappeared with her luggage and cape.

I looked around: The old gentleman was reading his twenty-seventh newspaper, the widow was on her tenth torte, the rain droned down on the skylights, and from the recess by the buffet below came the impersonal murmur of the barmaid with the waiters.

I glanced at her: That beautiful face was totally changed, obstinate and trembling, as she sipped hastily at her scalding tea.

"Come on," I said hoarsely, and took her hand.

"I asked if you were glad."

"No," I cried.

The old gentleman looked up from his paper, and the widow stopped chewing for a moment.

She laughed and followed me.

It was even quieter upstairs. The window in the room opened onto a light shaft, at the bottom of which ashes and rubbish lay soaking beside overflowing trash cans. The only sound was the crazed drone of the rain.

She sat on the bed and smoked, while I paced back and forth with my own cigarette. From time to time we glanced at each other, like people standing at the foot of a mountain, listening to the roar of an onrushing avalanche.

I remembered how I had kissed her in the dark vestibule of a large block of flats on the outskirts of town, where streetcars screeched their way to the end of the line, and in the light of an auto that rounded a corner, I saw her face, white and smiling against the rough brown wall.

“My God,” she said suddenly, “why all the moaning? Sit here beside me.” She smiled for the first time that day, then shoved the pillow over and made room for me.

“Give me your hand.”

I did. Her hands were cool and dry, very light. I felt her touch my wedding ring, then she put my hand back in my lap: My hand was heavy, almost dead.

“Let me go,” she said.

“Go,” I said.

Her lips brushed my hand.

I went to the window and waited. The rain was soaking a heap of ashes that had built up beside the trash can. Beneath the slender strands of yellowish rain a narrow, dirty channel of water flowed from the trash can toward a stopped-up drain. Scraps of paper drifted in a large puddle with peels and crushed cigarette butts, stringy bits of tobacco floating on the surface like small yellow worms. I flicked my own stub downward as well, then turned. The room was empty. I had heard nothing.

The Tribe of Esau

5

THAT HEEL, THE WOMAN THOUGHT, he's off again. He's escaped me and this filthy earth. He's gone. . . . She regarded the man with a bitter face. He lay half on his side; she saw his childlike, smiling profile, the mussed hair, and the half-bare arm. He had rolled up his sleeves and was holding a sheet of paper tightly in his right hand.

What a heel, she thought. He *is* a heel. He calls that work, he calls that life, nothing steady, no moderation, a life without order, the heel. Smiling like that.

She attempted to take the sheet of paper from him, but he grumbled angrily in his sleep and she quickly turned away, toward the hot-plate. The electric cord was defective, the Bakelite connection was broken, the prongs stuck in the hot-plate's socket every time as if they'd been glued, and if you pulled hard it damaged the coil, which was constantly going bad. Swearing softly, she repaired the coil, attached it to the hot-plate, and plugged it in. She waited for the coil to glow, holding her breath. It began to glow, and she put on the water. Then she began to straighten the room, rather noisily. It was a mess. He had soaked his feet and shaved before he started drinking; his things lay scattered about, the bowl filled with dirty water, the little mug with dried shaving cream stuck to the rim, his old socks, two hand towels, all scattered about the table, the chair, and the floor between the table and the chair.

Flowers stood on the desk; she removed the wilted ones and tossed them in the washbowl, added the water from the shaving mug, and emptied the whole thing into the rain gutter.

Heel, she thought, almost murmuring now, how long is he going to lie there. He calls that work.

She regarded him more closely. The room was tidy, the water was just starting to simmer, she had time. The look of happiness on his face almost drove her crazy; she hated that happiness. He doesn't get that happiness from me, she thought, he stole it somewhere. He prowls among the fragments of paradise and steals from their substance. And yet I love him. . . .

Abruptly, she tried to imagine him far away, in America or Australia, and her heart convulsed with fear that it might happen. I can't live without him, she thought, it's terrible. Even the pain he causes me makes me happy, the heel.

She pulled the chair over from the desk and sat down by the couch. Her feet hurt; she had walked a long way, looking for a place to borrow more money. No dice again. The last of the tea, she thought, the last of the butter and the last of the bread, and this heel is drunk again. I'd like to know what he wrote. . . .

She tried once more to pull the sheet of paper from his hand, very gently, but he grumbled again, and she was afraid to interrupt the natural course of his sleep. He hated being jerked from sleep. He always said it reminded him of the war: "Jerked from sleep! Sleep, one of God's most precious gifts."

She didn't have a penny, not a bit of credit left anywhere. No money for rent, for electricity—oh, why go over it all again.

She glanced at the hot-plate; the bubbling had subsided. She lifted the kettle with a curse. The coil was no longer glowing. She unplugged it, held her hand over the plate to check the heat, then began poking about on the coil, slowly and systematically, to see where the problem was this time. She cursed softly as she did so. She could feel her throat constricting to cry.

It was driving her crazy. Even if you had money, even if you tried to buy a new coil or a new hot-plate, or a new connection, you couldn't afford it. They asked ridiculous prices for items like that. And yet here you are going nuts over a connection, this shitty little piece of Bakelite, not worth twenty cents. Sighing, she lifted one tine of the fork—she'd discovered the break, it was hard to see, the coil had darkened and was brittle in several places. Almost every time it was used, it burned through in a new spot. She pulled on both ends of the wire coil and wrapped them around each other, then plugged it back in. It started to glow. She put the water on again.

It just makes me sick, she thought, the way they torment us. If I ever get hold of one of the guys who makes these Bakelite things or those coils, who drives thousands of men and women nuts, if I ever get hold of him, I'll murder him. . . . The water started bubbling again.

If he would only wake up. His face was so insanely happy it made her sick. She saw nothing of herself in his face. It was horrible to be so alone, to sit by his couch and not know what he had written, or whether it would be published, or if they would get any money for it. Not to know why he was smiling so happily, not to know where he found the money or the credit to get drunk. The bottle had tipped over next to the bed. She picked it up it and sniffed at it: Wine, she thought, red wine. . . .

The water seemed to be boiling. She lifted the lid, turned her face quickly from the billowing steam, and poured water in the teapot. Just a bit to warm the pot, then she set it back on the hot-plate. Tea water has to boil like mad, she thought, it has to get just as hot as it can. It has to be almost boiled to death.

She lifted the bottle again, sniffed at it once more, and replaced it carefully beside the couch. I love this heel, she thought. . . . I love him. She returned to the desktop with a sigh and lifted the lid again. The water was bubbling; she filled the pot, unplugged the hot-plate, and set the pot on the plate, which was still warm.

The Tale of Berkovo Bridge

THE TALE OF THIS BRIDGE was a lively topic of discussion at the time. Men cursed and wept over it, some laughed about it, some saw it as one of the countless events forming the general course of war, refusing to accord it any special significance—and indeed in the end the story was forgotten, since it was of no strategic or historic importance.

Yet I now feel obliged to tell what really happened on that decisive day. I've decided to tell things in chronological order, in as much detail as possible, for I suspect I may be the only one still living who played a major role. I know that Schnur and Schneider fell in battle, and I believe that their opposite number, a lieutenant from the staff of the Third Engineer Regiment, fell as well in the final months of the war, for I have sought him in vain. Or he may have wound up in prison, or dropped out of sight, or gone to the dogs, for who can say whether he might not have fallen prey to the general poison of the destruction, eking out a miserable existence, wandering about with no future, and no living connection to the past?

Since I'm going to try to keep things in strict sequence, I'll start with the day I received orders from Southeast Labor Pool Headquarters to take command of the construction—or better, reconstruction—of the bridge at Berkovo. It was a few days after Christmas, and I had been lounging about—with no project, although I longed for one—at KNX Reserve Construction Staff Headquarters. I was delighted finally to have something to do. Having requested and received the materials dealing with the project, I examined them methodically: The Berkovo Bridge had been blown up by a Russian rear-guard commando unit in the course of their retreat in 1941, shortly before the German arrival could prevent its destruction. The idea of rebuilding it was soon abandoned, since the small village of Berkovo had faded into strategic insignificance from both a military and a political point of view, particularly now that the bridge was no longer an important supply point. In the course of battle and the subsequent conquest, a military bridge had been constructed over the Berezina two kilometers to the southeast, which had since been reinforced and widened to serve as a supply line. The commanding officers of Southeast Construction and those of corresponding rank in the army deemed it more sensible at the time to use the materials, which would have been needed to rebuild the bridge at Berkovo, to construct the military bridge instead, particularly since—as I've already said—the market town of Berkovo was insignificant. In the course of the war it served only as a billet for a company of local defense reserves assigned to watch for rear-guard partisan activity.

That, in short, was the prehistory of the Berkovo Bridge.

A few days after Christmas in 1943, I received written orders to rebuild the bridge. I was promised all the men and material necessary for the job—whatever I thought it would take—and on first inspecting the site, I discovered the following: The small river of Berezina is approximately eighty meters wide at that point. The concrete-clad piers were still standing in the river, largely undamaged, while the bridge itself had been completely destroyed in expert fashion; the Berezina River had been washing around it for the past two and a half years. The tiny village of Berkovo consisted of about ten houses, of which five were still occupied or habitable; those remaining had fallen into disrepair over the years through lack of use, and the wood in them had been stripped away by soldiers of the local guard, no doubt for use in lighting the stoves and preparing meals. At the time I was taking my measurements and making the necessary calculations, four of the houses were occupied by the local guard, who were suffering from fatigue and relatively ineffective. An old Russian woman and her daughter lived in the fifth house; the two of them cooked, washed, and cleaned for the soldiers, and kept a tavern too, stocked from mysterious sources with schnapps, wine, and food.

I also came across a small graveyard where soldiers who had died or fallen in the line of duty over the years were buried. An exhumation squad was already in the process of digging up the corpses in order to rebury them in a planned cemetery for heroes of the Fatherland.

Together with my two closest colleagues, Schnur and Schneider, it took me barely three days to make the necessary measurements and calculations. From the time I made my first site inspection, I had devised a plan utilizing the existing concrete piers, bridging them over with an iron and wood superstructure, which, though not permanent, would last for three months or so, and would support even major troop movements with heavy armor. The word from Southeast Construction Headquarters was that the bridge would probably be used in the course of a general retreat, since command expected that the bridge two kilometers to the southeast would be heavily congested.

Of course, building a bridge slated for destruction the moment you've finished it is not a particularly rewarding task. Only the architect's profession places such strong emphasis on an object's durability, while other arts tend toward transience. So we made our measurements and calculations with no great joy, though we were certainly happy to have escaped the dull wait at KNX Reserve Construction Staff Headquarters.

Since my orders included instructions to complete the project within two weeks at the latest, and since I had reckoned on 3,000 man-days of labor, I requested 250 men, figuring in as usual an extra percentage for high work stoppage, wear and tear, and various other standard imponderables on projects of this nature. And naturally I needed at least fifty additional men as cooks, medics, and guards to handle the workers' mess hall, infirmary, and guard duty. A precondition was the ready availability of sufficient quantities of all the necessary building materials. And lastly, I needed a few explosives experts from the Corps of Engineers during the first two or three days to help blast away the few small remaining portions of the bridge itself.

All these calculations, measurements, and the like had taken the three of us—Schneider, Schnur, and me—roughly three days. During this first stay in Berkovo we had an opportunity to observe the rowdy, one might even say demoralized, behavior of the local reserve, who were under the command of an older second lieutenant and two sergeants. Rumors of the coming general retreat, which could no longer be silenced, had reached this godforsaken village and were running rampant.

Morale was sinking daily. Units making for the bridge on the basis of older maps often arrived by mistake, several trucks appeared carrying rations, and troops wandered in who had simply lost their way. The inevitable whispers that passed from man to man carried a message of cynical frankness: It's every man for himself. This was accompanied by a frightening and pernicious maxim: Enjoy the war; peace is going to be hell. These two precepts became standard mottoes of the local guard, who were expecting to be withdrawn any day. There was open prostitution with the tavern keeper's daughter, a coarse, crude blonde, as well as with other women. I myself saw large portions of the clothing depot and items of equipment (including, I presume, weapons) being sold or bartered to Russian vagabonds, who were literally dragging bags of money with them and disposing of the goods in some mysterious manner. There were orgies every night, in which the lieutenant, who raised a few feeble objections now and then, was placated expediently by shoving the best-looking woman present into his bed, after first making sure he'd had plenty to drink.

A certain strange sorrow clung to the soldiers in the midst of these activities, bearing witness to some remnant of decency; and it could perhaps be said that too much was asked of them. I must also add that a fairly large number of soldiers avoided these orgies; but two drunks make more noise than two hundred sober men. None of those who distanced themselves from such goings-on, however, were in a position to oppose them actively. They all suffered from the terrible sickness of resignation.

I reported such incidents the moment I returned to headquarters, as duty required, although I was aware of the difficulty I would have if I were asked, for example, to offer proof of my observations. It was standard practice in the course of a retreat for a unit to keep whatever black-market stock fell into its hands without reporting it.

Immediately upon my return I presented my plans and calculations, which were forwarded at once to the supply depot and labor pool department. Thanks to the admirable energy and high morale of our staff, the requested men and materials were not only made available but loaded and set in motion within the week. They even sent along four transportable barracks to house the men. These proved unnecessary upon arrival, since the local guard had been withdrawn in the meantime, so that the houses were now available. Since it would have been senseless to return the barracks, they simply made things more comfortable in the course of construction.

The South Army Group quickly deployed two panzer units to protect the now suddenly important bridge. These two units were posted approximately two hundred meters to the south and north of us, to protect us from possible surprise attacks from the hinterland as well as possible encroachments by Russian troops breaking through from the other bank of the river. A smaller troop took up position directly behind us, so that, protected by a sort of bridgehead, we were able to begin on schedule and according to plan.

I must add here that my people were extremely nervous, since the withdrawal of the local guard meant that for all practical purposes the area had returned to the status of a battlefield, and in fact based on the sounds of combat we heard over the next few days, at times relatively close, then farther off, we gathered that we were occupying a fairly advanced post.

But everything went according to plan, including the imponderables we had allowed for: work stoppages, loss of materials, unexpected disturbances in the course of construction, rain or extreme cold. The remaining piers had sustained greater damage than expected, for I hadn't been able to examine all of them closely during our initial inspection, no boat having been available. But we had made the necessary allowances, and our work proceeded on schedule. Early on I had the old woman who ran the tavern arrested, along with her daughter and the rest of that bunch, and requested new, supervised prostitutes, who arrived promptly and were billeted in one of the houses. We even managed to have schnapps and tobacco delivered, for over the years we had learned that these items, of relatively minor value in themselves, contributed significantly to the success of any project. After all, you couldn't expect willing and enthusiastic work from forced labor of all nationalities unless certain material advantages were made available to them.

Thus the two-week construction period proceeded according to schedule. The only thing worthy of note were the rumors delivered each day by the men driving the supply trucks: that a general retreat (now and then they even dared to use the word *rout*) was now underway; that a large number of our troops had already evacuated the right bank of the Berezina, which must mean they were planning to allow the main mass of the enemy to advance without resistance; that the bridge to the southeast would probably be sufficient for the retreat after all; all sorts of demoralizing tales to which I naturally closed my ears, even if they weren't truly mutinous enough to call for a military report. I remained in constant contact with headquarters, giving them regular reports on our progress, and it gave me a great deal of satisfaction not to have to make excuses about being behind on the project, since—as I've said—we were right on schedule.

It's true, however—and since I've made it my duty to report the truth, I must add this qualification—that I too was secretly disturbed by the sounds of battle, which had drawn fairly near after the first week and appeared to be approaching steadily ever since, at times coming dangerously close to the right bank of our construction project.

I was also allowing small groups of retreating soldiers to cross over on a footbridge, providing their papers were in order, or if they were accompanied by an officer, since I sympathized with these exhausted men and didn't want to send them two kilometers upstream unnecessarily. But in the case of leaderless and disorderly troops, or individuals who claimed to be stragglers, I was far stricter, insisting that they proceed to the other bridge, since I knew that they would be subjected to careful inspection there and that no one fleeing on his own, or perhaps even planning to desert, would be allowed to cross. The gloomy silence of the officers in these groups, seven or eight of whom I allowed to cross during the first ten days or so, reinforced in me a certain inner pessimism, of which of course I gave no external sign. I was relieved of all personal responsibility by my daily contact with Southeast Construction Headquarters, who constantly emphasized the importance of finishing the bridge on schedule.

Thus everything proceeded according to plan, right up to the final day of construction. Two days before the deadline we were already beginning to affix the thick, treated oak planks to the finished framework of the rebuilt bridge with a special type of threaded rivet. These thick planks could support the heaviest of vehicles and armored weapons. Work progressed well on the final day. Knowing we were near our goal put everyone in a good mood, and the prospect of soon escaping the danger zone—the noise of distant battle from retreating troops could now be heard both night and day—spurred everyone on. I had half the planks we needed carried across the footbridge to the other side of the river—taking responsibility for the risk, having prudently considered the probable success of the measure—so that we could begin laying the planks from both directions on the final day. This introduced a certain healthy competition between the two teams working on the bridge, leaving aside the motivating factors already mentioned above. Over the years I'd often found such competitive situations useful. A total of 120 workers were involved, and I had divided them into two teams of sixty each, under the command of Schnur and Schneider. The remaining eighty—the others had dropped out, as predicted—had been ordered to start loading the unused construction supplies, as well as the tools, kitchen utensils, and so on, for my ambition was to inform the Southeast Construction Headquarters of the completion of the bridge and of our total readiness to withdraw in a single call.

Around noon on the final day the teams had drawn so near to one another that I could extend the work break by half an hour with an easy mind (much against the wishes of the men, as I later learned, who would have preferred to work on to the end without a break, in order to escape the increasingly risky situation). The apparent eagerness and exhaustion of the men made me lenient, however. I was filled with the proud knowledge that we were reaching the end of a skillfully calculated project, carried out with equally masterful speed and precision. My commanding officers at headquarters, who had inspected the ongoing project on several occasions in the company of various members of the general's staff, let it be known that I was assured of the Distinguished Service Medal, First Class.

Work continued rapidly after the break, and good progress was being made in loading the supplies. I had already dispatched several trucks.

The noise of battle was constant, and now it came nearer, seeming to concentrate menacingly at a single spot. The sound of heavy cannon reached us like someone pounding steadily and impatiently on a door, trying to break it down, and at times we could hear not only the impact of the shells but also the discharge of the guns. All of these sounds, including infantry fire and the rumble of tanks, accompanied the final hours of our work, but could not prevent it. To be sure, the panzer units deployed for our protection—without having received any orders, as I later learned—made ready to withdraw, and both commanding officers, a lieutenant and a captain, kept a silent eye on the construction site, probably to get some idea as to when their flight might commence.

I was first directly affected when, around three in the afternoon, a young second lieutenant from the engineer brigade drove up in an all-terrain vehicle, accompanied by two soldiers. This very likable and sensible young man told me that he had been ordered to blow up the bridge at four o'clock. He showed me his written orders, and delivered news of recent strategic developments to justify his assignment. The retreat of the troops on the opposite bank was now almost complete. One of the larger units had been left behind to engage the main body of the enemy and give the appearance of major resistance. Of course, the lieutenant told me in confidence, the unit had secretly been given up for lost, and the order had been issued to blow up both bridges at four o'clock, regardless of the situation at the time.

Two enemy army columns were expected to arrive at the respective bridges around four-thirty at the latest, and the Army Command Staff felt they could not afford to leave either bridge open as a line of retreat for the troops who were still fighting, fearing that either bridge might be taken by the enemy and used in their advance. So the order had been given to blow them up by four o'clock at the latest, sooner if necessary. Still, this was not to be done until enemy troops were observed in the immediate vicinity. This would place us in an extremely disadvantageous position, however, since the forest stretched almost to the water along the right bank of the Berezina.

First I inspected the bridge, which was now almost finished, with the young lieutenant, and during this initial inspection, which took place around three-fifteen, he sought out the best locations for the explosives. He was amazed at the state of the bridge. He'd been told it would be at least another week before the bridge at Berkovo would be finished, and he knew the same impression had been conveyed to the officers of the troops battling on the other side. This offered sufficient explanation for the surprising fact that not a single unit of regular troops had tried to cross the bridge up to this point. Even in its present condition it could have served as a crossing, even for motorized units, and I certainly wouldn't have stopped anyone from using it.

I returned at once to my office and, in the presence of the

lieutenant, began a fruitless series of phone calls. I called the commanders at Construction Headquarters: They'd heard nothing about blowing up the bridge. I was to continue construction until I received orders to the contrary. Then it took me almost half an hour to reach the Southeast High Command, over lines that had been heavily damaged. The lieutenant's orders were confirmed.

My situation was, as may be imagined, a strange one. Everything the lieutenant said appeared valid, and although I would have given a good deal to complete my project, I had no interest in placing even the least of my men at risk for a single moment longer than my orders required. I therefore phoned again to Construction Headquarters. Like Command Headquarters, they were located approximately two hundred kilometers to the west. The chief himself ordered me rather impatiently to continue construction, as a matter of principle. His exact words were: We mustn't abandon our principles, no matter how much pressure we're under. Then he added that he was expecting to hear from Command Headquarters any minute with confirmation of the lieutenant's orders. He hung up. It was ten minutes to four. The bridge would be finished by four, and an ominous silence reigned on the other side of the river. The bridge was complete except for a remaining gap of about three-quarters of a meter. It would be finished precisely to the minute. Not one of my projects had ever proved untenable. I tested the solidity of the planks and rivet screws one last time. In the meantime all the remaining supplies had been loaded, and only a few empty trucks stood waiting for the workers, their motors running. I had given orders to withdraw at five past four.

Two men from Schneider's team screwed down the last of the rivets a few minutes before four, while the lieutenant was already busy placing the explosives, which were linked by fuses. The lieutenant himself walked to the middle of the bridge at one minute to four, where I was watching the last of the planks being fastened onto the frame. He asked me not to screw down the final plank, since it was a perfect location for a charge of explosives, but I insisted on it, since I had received explicit orders from the chief to stick to our principles. The lieutenant shrugged and walked off. I glanced again at the bridge, then returned to the construction hut with Schnur, Schneider, and the last of the workers to register the completion of the bridge at Berkovo precisely on schedule.

But now something horrifying happened. On the other side, in the breathless silence, fleeing soldiers appeared from the woods, a few carrying wounded men, others racing along singly, in spite of the total exhaustion that could be read in their faces at this short distance; vehicles too emerged from the woods, all in fearful, wild flight. The crowd thickened, streaming from the forest, racing for the bridge, which must have appeared like hope incarnate, since I had ordered a swastika flag attached to its highest point to celebrate its completion.

The lieutenant now rushed from the bridge with his men, shrugged, and showed me his watch, which indicated five seconds to four, pointing with his other hand toward a few Russian tanks firing at the fleeing men and drawing dangerously near to the bridge.

The moment I saw the burning fuse, I too ran to my office and tried to call Southeast Construction Headquarters as quickly as possible. But before my call had gone through, another phone rang. I lifted the receiver and heard the chief's voice: Stop work on the bridge at once. And since he was about to hang up, I cried "Hold it!" and gave my report according to regulations: construction of the bridge completed on schedule, to the minute, as ordered. But he was no longer listening . . . and I was almost deafened by the savage blast with which the bridge now exploded into the air. Then I went to my car and ordered everyone to move out. But I can't tell you what the bridge at Berkovo looked like after the explosion, because I didn't look back, although the shells of the Russian tanks were already landing among the houses of Berkovo. Yet sometimes I think I see those exhausted, fleeing men who fought to the last, protecting us too, as duty demanded, and although I did not actually see them, I see them cursing, the fear of death upon their faces, the fear of capture, and hate for us as well, although we too did nothing but act as duty demanded.

The Dead
No Longer Obey

THE LIEUTENANT TOLD US TO take a break and we did. We were at the edge of a forest, the sun was shining, it was springtime, everything was quiet, and we knew the war would soon be coming to an end. Those with tobacco lit up and the rest of us tried to get some sleep. We were tired, having eaten little and carried out several counterattacks over the past three days. It was marvelously peaceful, somewhere birds were singing, and the air was filled with a soft, moist tenderness.

Suddenly the lieutenant starting shouting. He cried out: "Hey!" Then he grew angry and bellowed: "Hey, you!" Finally, becoming furious, his voice broke: "You! You there! You!"

Then we saw who he was yelling at. Someone was sitting on the other side of the woodland road, asleep. It was an ordinary soldier, dressed in gray, leaning back against a tree, asleep. The soldier had a pleasant smile on his freckled face, and we thought the lieutenant would go nuts. We thought the soldier was nuts too, because the lieutenant kept on shouting and the sleeping man kept right on smiling.

The men who had started to smoke stopped, the ones trying to sleep were now wide awake, and some of us were smiling, too. The spring air was fresh and gentle, and we knew that the war would soon be over.

Suddenly the lieutenant stopped shouting and jumped up.

He crossed the road in two long strides and struck the sleeping man in the face.

We saw now that the sleeping man was dead. He fell over without a word, no longer smiling. His face was affixed with a terrible grin, and we didn't feel at all sorry for the lieutenant, who came back pale faced, for the sun no longer gave us pleasure. We found no joy in the soft moisture of the mild spring air, and it made little difference to us now whether the war was coming to an end or not. Suddenly we felt we were all dead—the lieutenant too, for he was grinning now, and no longer wore a uniform.

America

9

I FOUND HUBERT LYING IN his bed, which he had shoved closer to the stove. He had kindled a pathetic fire from a few old picture frames. Of course it couldn't heat the huge room. A tiny island of a somewhat humane temperature surrounded the stove, but elsewhere the room, with all its paintings, easel, and cupboards, lay cold and poignantly desolate. Hubert was holding a sketch on his knees that he'd just begun, but he was no longer working on it, gazing meditatively instead at some vague spot on the brown bedspread. He greeted me with a smile, laid the drawing aside, and in his sad, large gray eyes, I read for the moment only hunger and scant hope. But I didn't leave him stretched on the rack for long; instead I pulled out some fresh, sweet-smelling, white bread. His eyes gleamed.

"Either you're crazy," he said, "or I am. Or you've stolen this, or I'm dreaming, or . . ." He made a dismissive gesture and rubbed his eyes. "It's simply not true."

"Look," I said, holding it under his nose, pressing it into his hands, making the crisp crust crackle. "Now you've touched it, experienced it with all your senses. Think you're crazy for all I care, but I certainly didn't steal it. Cut it in two, would you?"

Hubert finally seemed to trust his senses, seized the bread firmly, as if he feared he were reaching into the void, realized that it was real, then pulled the knife from the cupboard with a strange groan. Meanwhile I had pulled the tobacco from my pocket and was cutting the plug into smaller pieces, which I crumbled and placed on the warm stove plate. They call it roasting, I believe. Hubert gazed at me with shining eyes, sniffed greedily, and said: "You've turned into a regular criminal."

We ended up stretched out beside each other on the bed, each of us enjoying our portion of bread, pinching small pieces from the loaf and stuffing them in our mouths, sweet-smelling bread, fresh and still warm, white and delicious. Bread is the best thing there is. Woe unto the man who no longer eats bread because he is full. Woe!

I was happy that Hubert had apparently forgotten the question of where the bread came from. My God, if he'd insisted on knowing. He's so strict about things, a true artist! But he ate silently, happily; ah, happy the man who still has a bit of bread.

"Do you know what I was thinking when you came in?"

I had to admit I didn't. I'm not a psychologist, for God's sake.

"I was wondering, if American universities ran some experiments, I was wondering how many calories they'd find in a genius, in Rembrandt for instance. After all, modern science can tell us anything. What do you think?"

"Maybe they'd discover that a genius lives beyond the norm. That he eats a tremendous amount or starves himself, that his accomplishments are independent of—let's say—his so-called caloric intake."

"But even a genius has a starvation limit. He might starve and freeze all week in a cellar for all I care, and still write a wonderful sonnet. But if you spend your whole life in a cold cellar, it's all over with the sonnet writing, over because you simply no longer have the strength to write sonnets with a pencil stub on some dirty piece of paper."

"But I would claim he might have many, many beautiful unwritten sonnets in his mind, sonnets the world will never see, although they're there, sonnets which might be *immortal* were they known."

Our bread was finished. I reached from the bed and gathered the roasted tobacco from the stove, filled our pipes, and Hubert held out a piece of his drawing as a spill. I lit it at the stove and now we smoked as dusk fell in the large room, creeping in like fog, enveloping everything.

"I'll write to America," said Hubert, "and see if they'll try to figure out Rembrandt's daily calorie intake." He looked at me uneasily. "I have an inferiority complex because I can't work as long as I used to. And I read recently in the newspapers that they've run tests in America showing that at our caloric level a person can't do creative work—at least not two years' worth. This major scientific discovery has depressed me so much I can't paint anymore."

Suddenly he sprang out of bed like a wild man, right past me, raced to the easel, stretched a sheet of paper on the board, and began working like crazy. He dashed off a lively sketch, grabbed the box of watercolors, and was off, with strong, bold strokes, stepping back from time to time to judge the effect. He finished a small painting I couldn't see clearly because it was getting darker and darker in the room. But all at once he turned around and asked me energetically: "Where did you get the bread, you bastard?"

I had to show my colors at last. "I traded my pen for it," I said shyly, "to an American soldier. Here." I pulled the two white cylinders from my pocket, "there's a cigarette for each of us too."

We laid aside our smelly pipes at once and inhaled the marvelous tobacco with deep enjoyment—American cigarettes! Hubert worked boldly on; he had turned on the light.

"The best thing about America, the very best thing of all, are the cigarettes," he said with a laugh.

Paradise Lost

THE FORMER PATHS WERE SCARCELY visible in the tangled shrubbery, in part no longer even recognizable. The broken gaps of the fence admitted one and all, the luxuriant greenery had been trampled flat, wilted, rotted, replaced by new growth, until at last a sort of gauzy jungle had rendered the untended paths impassable. New ones had been ruthlessly flattened, no longer following any plan, but simply the dictates of convenience, and now led to the house from all different directions. Even the old main road, which had bordered the park in a half circle, was scarcely passable. Seams of grass had spread from the sides toward the middle, meeting to form sparse new grassy areas in which stripling elders, box trees, and elder bushes were growing merrily, the decayed banks covered with foliage. The fountain at the upper curve of the path was covered with moss and filled with dirt and tin cans, so that in spite of the wet spring weather, it held scarcely a drop of water. Its iron water spout had been bent by a well-aimed rock, and I discovered signs of children at play, who, digging through the decayed vegetation, had produced a hole at the base of which a thick, greenish fluid was visible. Next I saw that the large, graveled square had been dug up and planted, and that the rocks and gravel had been swept together and dumped into the fountain. A poorly patched fence surrounded a few miserable cabbages, which had been given ample time to rot over the course of the winter. Wilted bean stalks clung to water pipes, and from a few inevitable tin buckets rose the stench of a greenish liquid similar to that which evidently lay hidden beneath the fountain.

At last I came upon a person. Behind some sort of shed, which probably held gardening tools, sat an old man on a crate, a spade propped between his knees, a pipe in his mouth. But even though the gentle, veiled afternoon of my homecoming left me longing for a human face, I was still taken aback when I saw one. I retreated a few steps so that the shed again hid him from view, and only then did I look around.

The former layout of the park could be clearly discerned from this vantage point. The handsome large semicircle, once covered with white gravel, was now traversed by pathetic fences constructed out of narrow strips of stamped tin, warped by rust and ready to break, gas pipes, and box-tree branches. Yet the square still retained the soft, fertile beauty of perfection, even though its once smooth and carefully tended shrub border was now tangled, cut, burned, and trampled. Archaeologists say nothing is more indestructible or more easily found, even centuries later, than a hole, something dug into the earth, and this beautifully designed park was still wholly present in form.

Higher up, at the top of the curve of the clear half circle, lay the round, soiled, but still perfect circle of the fountain, from which the main road led straight to the entrance gate. And in the bearded, greenish, curling undergrowth of the shrubbery the small paths that could scarcely be seen up close were now clearly apparent, indelibly preserved like smooth weals in the foundering, arched backs of the shrubbery, while to the left and right of the main road ran the other two, simple and clear, in the shape of musical clefs.

And now at last I dared to look at the house. I saw it clearly through the gaps in the row of poplars, with their gleaming, thick, fresh-green foliage. I counted the trees; seven of twelve remained, while the willows at either end were still undamaged. The facade of the house, with its gray and intentionally somewhat rough surface, was practically unaltered. A few large patches of plaster had fallen here and there, and large, grayish white water spots appeared in a few places, like the cover of an old, damp-stained book. Only a few of the windows still contained unbroken glass; most were covered instead with millboard or nailed shut with plywood, while others were partially bricked up and inset with windows too small for the grand casements.

For the moment I was only registering visual impressions. The memories were too numerous, the feelings too powerful, for me to allow them to rise. Although everything—past, memory, youth, and life—bound me to this house and park, I could only stand like a stranger visiting some outlying area of fine homes, who, overcome by simple curiosity, bypasses a gate now rusted shut and steps into the garden through a gap in the fence, to view the traces of destruction.

Painfully we recognize the inner transformations that mark the threshold of maturity. With ineffable sorrow we leave behind the toys and playgrounds of childhood, plunging with fear, sorrow, and desire into that tumult the grown-ups have always called life; more sadly yet do we leave the house of youth, the place of dreams, sensing darkly that our memories are but memories of dreams, already tasting the unspeakable pain we will feel when we are no longer simply adults, but old, and for the first time we glimpse ahead the only moment of which we can be sure, the one in which we cross the threshold of death to enter into another life.

The roof of the house was only partially covered by the old, dark gray tiles. It must have been badly damaged, for large portions were now nailed over with patches of roofing felt or tin, and partly with brightly colored advertising signs, and even outside the tiny attic window I saw a drying rack, from which dismal gray diapers flapped wearily in the slack breeze. At the left corner of the house a section of the gutter was hanging down, just as it had seven years earlier, when I stood at this spot and took my leave. Back then I thought: They'll have to have it repaired; I didn't think: I must leave now, and I don't know if I'll ever return. I thought: They'll have to have it repaired. But they hadn't; it was still hanging there—one of the clamps attaching it to the edge of the roof had come loose, and it hung there at an angle, ready to fall at any moment, and I could see clearly where the water poured at an angle against the gray side of the building each time it rained, rushing down, soaking it, a white path edged in dark gray trailing down past the windows, with large round spots to the left and right, their centers white, with increasingly darker rings about them.

That section of gutter had been dangling there for seven years. Seven years. I had traveled far, I had seen death many times, smelled and felt it. I had lived luxuriously, had hungered, starved to the point where I dreamed of white bread, imagining how I would tear into it, bury my face in it, share it, toss it to the entire starving world. I had starved to the point where I no longer felt hunger, but was wrapped instead in those sweet dreams that make actual eating—when it begins again—seem unspeakably disgusting. I had been shot at thousands of times, by guns, mortars, cannons, ships' artillery, airplanes, bombs, and hand grenades. I'd been hit, I'd tasted my own blood on my lips, flowing stickily from my head, sweet and greasy, quickly thickening. I had marched along dusty roads all over Europe until I could no longer feel my feet, pursued white-throated women through dark suburbs without ever, ever possessing a single one; oh, those white throats in dusky lanes. . . .

So very much had happened to me in that time, and it shocked me to think that this damaged gutter had been hanging here those same seven years, guiding the rain at an angle against the facade of the house. This piece of tin had dangled on what remained of its clamp for seven years, roof tiles had blown off, trees had been uprooted, plaster had crumbled, and bombs had fallen from all sides on the sweet open flanks of the city, in the suburbs, woven about with greenery, but this small piece of tin had never been hit, nor forced by a blast of wind to abandon its angle and fall to the ground. Rain had fallen heavily in those seven years, but it had splashed against the facade of the house, had been absorbed by the porous, sandstone wall, and had emerged again, whitish and gray.

Through the gaps in the row of poplars allowing a clearer view of the house, I could see wash hanging out on windy racks: faded men's shirts, frayed women's linen, sweaters, red and green, dresses, and among them a wet, heavy blanket that seemed to pull down on the rack like a leaden weight. Nothing familiar remained, and I was glad. I had always hated the house, loving only its inhabitants, and although the old forms of the park and house emerged everywhere like the watermark of eternity, I was most deeply affected by that flimsy piece of tin hanging at an angle above the pockmarked frieze of baby angels supporting the roof.

For some time now I had noticed a shadow at the edge of my vision: the man who was sitting on the bench. Evidently he had risen and walked around the corner of the shed, and I now realized that he must have been standing at the edge of my field of vision for some time—whether for minutes, seconds, or hours I couldn't have said—like a small gray speck of dust when you're too busy looking to wipe it from your eye. I turned around again, taking in the park with a sweeping glance, particularly the shrubbery, deeply and painfully reminded of those two stone benches hidden at the thickest point of the musical-clef paths. Then I turned to the admonishing shadow waiting humbly in my field of vision and advanced a few paces.

Up to that point I had passed through the garden plots wherever there was a gap in a fence without thinking, since I could see no sign of planting or sowing. Now I crossed a tiny field of corn stubble along a narrow path and made my way the few paces to the shed.

It seemed as if I had crossed an acoustic border with those three strides. As soon as I was standing beside the man, who nodded in a friendly fashion and returned my "Good evening" with the same words, I heard the sound of children playing, women calling out, men whistling, all the indescribable sounds of evening leisure in the neighborhood of a crowded house on a spring evening after work. Radios warbled lightheartedly through the air, and at the main entrance to the house, which now lay directly before me, I saw two older girls playing with red balls beside the large sandstone pillars of the door. And now I saw for the first time that the left wing of the house had been hit by a heavy shell, and the hole filled in with ugly, blackish bricks. Small children were playing in a sand pile between the poplar trunks, others were striking each other with sticks, running about and screaming with laughter, and a man had turned his bicycle upside down to work on it with rolled-up sleeves.

The old man beside me had seated himself on a board hastily nailed to two wooden blocks, and I sat down beside him. He was short and thin, and although he was wearing a threadbare sailor's cap, I could see from his bare temples and the completely hairless visible portions of his skull that he must be bald. His narrow face was nicely tanned, and his small, almost colorless eyes regarded me with good-natured curiosity. I had been beside him barely half a second before he seemed to sense that I was eagerly inhaling the aroma of his tobacco. Without a word, he started searching through his pockets, while I immediately felt for my pipe.

"I don't have a paper," he said, holding out a tobacco tin.

"Thanks," I said, took the tin, opened it quickly, and filled my pipe.

"Need a light?" he asked.

I nodded.

"Thanks," I said again, handing the tin back to him.

"You're from . . ."

"France," I said.

"That's what I was about to say; you can always tell by certain features. Rough time?"

I nodded.

"Right."

It felt good to smoke a pipe with someone, the mutual movements of the lips, a smacking motion, and the gentle, almost inaudible puffs with which, in tandem, the blue clouds of smoke are expelled that come gray from the lungs.

I no longer saw much. I suddenly knew that the old man would ask what they all do, and that I would have to say no. I was worried when he started to speak, but all he said was: "Are you looking for someone?"

"Yes," I said softly.

"Who?"

"Family. Fräulein Maria X."

"Oh," he cried, and although he was sitting so close beside me that I would never forget the smell of his clothes, I felt him withdraw. "The Fräulein!"

He must have sensed the rapid, irregular pounding of my heart, he may have seen the drops of sweat breaking out on my brow, and he was surely astonished to see me remove the pipe from my mouth, hold the bowl in my hand, and sigh deeply. Then he drew nearer and said softly, but more coldly than anything he had said thus far: "Don't worry, she's here."

"Thanks," I said, sticking the pipe back in my mouth. I knew now that I had plenty of time, all the time in the world, and I was surprised myself at the depth of the sigh that emerged from me, without my knowledge or will.

Now I felt the old man scrutinizing my worn and tattered uniform; I sensed him drawing a bit closer and closed my eyes, because I knew what he would ask me now.

"Maybe you know him." he said.

I said nothing.

"He was a corporal. Grittner. Hubert. My son. Western front like you. Maybe you know him."

"Where?" I asked hoarsely.

"Falaise," he said, and I felt him waiting. . . .

"I was there too," I said, and now I looked at him. He had removed his pipe from his mouth, wrapping his right hand around the warm bowl, and in his compressed lips and narrowed eyes stood the certainty that he would learn nothing from me. "No," I said with a sigh, and shook my head. Then I put the pipe back in my mouth and looked toward the house.

"Funny," he said, "so many have come back, and not a single one has known him." I started to say something, but he raised his pipe and cut me off. "Oh, I know," he said. "A name means nothing. At Verdun you seldom knew the person lying a foot away from you, I know all about it."

He interrupted himself, looking up as a young, cheerful voice called from the house: "Dad!"

"Yes," he called out softly, "I'm coming," and he touched the rim of his cap with his pipe stem, said good-bye, and left. I called him back and asked: "Which room is she in?"

He understood me at once and pointed with his pipe toward the room next to the dangling gutter.

"Thanks," I said and watched as he headed for the house. He walked, as always, no doubt, slowly and calmly, with a slight stoop. He knocked his pipe on the stone lion, which stood halfway along the row of poplars, then turned and nodded to me once again, and in those few seconds it took him to reach the dark entrance and disappear within it, in those few seconds, I suddenly realized that *we all* are guilty *of everything.* Nothing touches us, for when we're asked about someone, we say no. We always have to say no, and when we say it, our hearts refuse to break, when, in fact, what we are saying is: Am I my brother's keeper?

I knew she wasn't there, but I suddenly stood and followed the old man into the house. I entered without taking a close look, but even in passing through I saw, sensed, and smelled that the house looked as if a company of soldiers had spent three weeks there. The staircase was almost undamaged, missing only a lath here and there, and the upper story was dark. I saw at once that the side windows had been boarded up, the light stood in stiff, silver-gray stripes along the edges of the boards, and the hall gave the impression of a cold, rainy, gray winter day outside, with a leaden sky by evening, followed by a sad and starless night.

And although I knew that she wasn't there, I walked quickly to the end of the hall, knocked, waited, knocked again, and rattled the door handle. Naturally nothing stirred, nor did anything stir within me, and in the half minute I stood there, I kept asking myself why that was. The fact that she had kept this same room said a great deal, said everything. But I felt nothing. Finally I noticed a note attached to the door. I tore it off and read it in the light seeping into the hall through the cracks of the old, musty boards.

It was her handwriting: *Be back at eight. Key next door. M.* I stuck the note in my pocket and knocked at the neighboring door. I had heard nothing before I knocked, but now an oppressive silence weighed upon my heart, as if someone were pumping air into me, pressing tighter and tighter against it. I knocked again, then I heard whispering, someone rose from a bed, a key turned in the lock, and in the flat dimness I saw the head of a pretty blond woman, her hair hanging in her eyes. Although I saw only a small strip of her throat, I knew that she was naked. I could smell it as well.

"Fräulein X," I said, "the key for Fräulein X . . ."

"Oh," she cried out, "You're the one whose picture is hanging over the bed."

"Yes," I said, "probably so."

She closed the door quickly, I heard more whispers, and then a round, naked, and very pretty arm held out a key to me.

I went back, and during the three steps to the door, in the musty hall, which still looked like winter, I realized that there was no point in holding back the memories any longer, once I was in the room. I stuck the key in the lock, paused for a moment, and crumpled the note in my pocket into a tight, small mass, so that I could feel it between my fingers like a tiny, hard paper ball.

Back then it seemed I could see nothing but the part in her hair. It was below me, straight and neat, white and steep like a very narrow, wonderfully bright pathway between soft, gently rising and falling waves of light brown hair. My gaze fell down that part and was lost forever. That narrow pathway had no end, and I felt the sorrow in my heart for that part in her hair.

He could feel her heart beating against his right side, softly and steadily, and knew it was a good heart, with more love in it for him than he would ever find elsewhere. He knew all these things back then, knew he was so close to her he could never, ever be closer. The window stood half open as the dewy, sweet fragrance of the park, filled with enchanting decay, drifted into the room. The greenish curtain colored the light, dying her scattered clothes on the floor a similar green. The carpet and chest of drawers, the chair where his sword belt lay, everything was dusky green, tender and beautiful; even the cheap silver buckle of his belt was tinged with green, and he could read the raised inscription surrounding the national insignia and the laurel-wreath clearly: GOD IS WITH US. At the sight of her linen, the brown skirt and red sweater, an infinite tenderness swept over him. He suddenly understood why men promise to fetch the stars from heaven for a woman. His service jacket lay spread out so that only the inner lining was visible, and part of the shoulder straps, bordered in white, and he saw that the collar-band was soiled. But his happily wandering gaze continued to return to the relentlessly clear and neat part in her hair lying below him, and he knew that this pathway had no end, that he would never come as near to any other human as he had to her. Yet she was as infinitely distant as the pathway of the part in her hair was long.

He felt her warm nose against his chin and her breath on his throat, and he sensed that she would never, ever stir again, if he himself did not stir.

Still holding the key, which was already in the lock, he felt the tiny, wadded note in his hand. He chewed his lower lip as he recalled the voice of the woman next door saying: "Oh, you're the one whose picture is hanging over the bed." She started singing, and he could hear her pause in her song to take a deep breath, and then a man's voice could be heard.

He too wished never to stir again back then, to gaze repeatedly down the ravine of that pathway, at times to strip off his clothes, which lay like the flayed green skins of strange beings on the floor, to hear her heart beating against his right side, softly and steadily, a good heart, a happy heart, a better heart than he could ever hope to find, and to feel her warm nose on his chin and her gentle breath flowing at regular intervals against his throat like the breath of a child.

At times he rested his head upon her forehead, and then he could see, on the dark walls, the large, heavy, beautiful painting attributed to Rubens, the shimmering, bright pink flesh of a woman, overly alive against the dark green walls. But this woman had silver-gray hair, which now looked green as well, and her gracious, slight smile passed over both of them, far into the distance. And when he gazed upward while resting on her forehead, he saw the tops of the poplars, silver-gray and near, smelled their cool, astringent fragrance, and through the gaps he saw in the far, far distance the edge of town, red roofs, the trees' bright foliage, the pale towers of the new churches, the black ones of the old, and recalled that it was autumn, in wartime.

He saw everything and nothing. The pattern in the carpet,

an eternally self-renewing meander of colors, crossing, overlapping, recrossing, overlapping again, and at the points of intersection large, brightly colored flowers, the tiny spots of damage on the light brown dressing table, and a small, alluringly bright hole in her stocking, which lay in the middle of the room, a tiny green hole. While he saw everything, he saw nothing but the boundless distance at the end of the part in her hair, inaccessible.

It was so quiet, war seemed impossible. In the halls outside, beyond the pale yellow door, the same warm friendliness reigned that they found in the face of the reclining Rubens. Their gaze passed beyond her to the park outside. The sublime, expansive, luxurious fragrance of autumn gathered at the half-open window, a splendid, total silence hovered in the air, enveloping a room that no one would ever enter or leave again, if such was their wish.

Yet he knew it was not only autumn, but wartime. From the moment reason returned, as his gaze followed the lovely, bright, narrow pathway of the part in her hair, he knew that he would have to rise, leave, and return again, and he feared returning most of all. He knew that the soiled collar-band of his uniform would soon be around his neck, that he would face their snarls, his face impassive, and he had a momentary vision of the distant outline of the city, shaved bare, towerless, flat like the sterile silhouette of a churchless village.

Suddenly he felt the soft touch of her lashes on his cheek, knew that she had opened her eyes, and realized that he was naked. Then he saw her hair close up, the short part in her hair, and beyond it the white pillow. As if he were recovering consciousness, everything drew closer, like a field glass coming into focus. He smelled the garden, redolent and cloud-covered, smelled her skin and heard the soft murmur of voices on the terrace below, heard the clinking of glasses and the full, baroque laughter of a woman. And he realized that all those sitting below knew about them, and that no one would say anything.

He saw in detail what he would be doing in a few minutes. Saw himself dressing, kissing her forehead, quietly leaving the room, disappearing through the rear gate, never to return again.

And in the same instant he realized that he was naked, he pictured her rising that next morning and going downstairs, without a question raised, until one day someone would mention with a smile that the postwoman was certainly bringing a lot of letters, and later he'd seen her a thousand times, running up the stairs with his letters, jerking open the door, leaning back against it, and tearing them open, her hands trembling.

And as he passed through the back entrance, through that rusty, creaking, iron gate, he knew that he would never fear death, but only life.

He released the crumpled note, felt his hands sweating, then turned the key and entered the room.

He walked quickly across the carpet, past the bed, which still stood on the right near the window, and looked toward the window, which opened onto the park: The light entered the room only through the narrow slits of the closed shutters, slicing the space into individual, closely layered planes. The room was saturated with bands of light, separated from each other by thin strata of shadow. Everything he could see was striped light and dark, and there could be no doubt that it was all real. The painting was still on the wall, still too bright and too alive for the dark green wallpaper, the stripes crossing the face, the dresser and bed, and he caught a glimpse of a large glass case overflowing with odds and ends, and a desk between the bed and door. All was dark below the level of the window ledge, illuminated only faintly by the reflection of those stripes of light and shadow, and he gathered from a burning smell the presence of a stove. But he noted all this merely in passing. He had intended to walk over, throw open the window, and take possession of the room, but after the first step he'd sensed something strange, immaterial, insubstantial, ineffable, that reminded him the room was not his. And that it would be equally difficult for him to take possession of either her or the room. Something foreign, unknown, filled him with a jealousy he'd not felt before. The moment he was touched by that shadowy, transitory, but unspeakably real presence, a savage, raging jealousy stabbed deep into his heart, and he knew that far from fearing to have her, he would instead have to fight for her.

He paused for a moment just beyond the threshold, wondering whether to turn on the light, to seek some clue, some concrete object that might possibly explain this sense of strangeness and fright, but he knew at once that it would be nothing tangible or visible, or even connected to tangible, visible objects, and that he had no right to seek such things, even if they existed.

He walked out slowly and relocked the door.

The dialogue of male and female voices next door was louder

and clearer now. He even understood a few words, but they rained down like shells falling short.

A door was abruptly opened somewhere in the rear of the house, and for a moment the dimly lit hall filled partially with gray light; other doors opened and shut again, steps faded down a wooden stairway, and now he smelled the distinct odor of fish and sliced onions. He leaned against the door frame. Now he understood what it meant: Her heart had been beating for twenty-five years, but he'd only felt it beat for half a minute, her brain had been thinking for twenty-five years, millions of thoughts, and he'd only known a fraction of them. He'd thought he possessed her, possessed her so thoroughly he could never lose her, so much so, so strongly, that he was afraid to return. Now he understood how senseless and silly he had been to believe that. He knew nothing about her, nothing he could call his own. He might just as well dip a pail in the ocean and claim he owned the sea. He didn't even know what she liked to eat, where she lived or how. He tried to imagine her riding the tram, looking out at passersby, stores, animals, buildings, piles of rubble, flowers and trees, tried to imagine each thought that connected her to all these things, to flowers, trees, animals, people, and stores. Her every thought, dozens every minute, was a world in itself, and there were a million such worlds in her, memories, dreams. He knew so infinitely little of it all that he felt totally miserable, leaning back against the door frame in this dark hall, which smelled increasingly of fish and onions, and now began to reek of vinegar, too.

Jealousy raged like a savage beast that had crept inside him and was now tearing him apart. How he wanted to possess her as he had back then, totally, yet knowing that the smooth pathway of the part in her hair was endless and that he could never travel to its end. How he hated her shoelace; he tried to imagine it: a brown, slightly frayed shoelace, on the end of which some dirt had perhaps dried. She had always been slightly unkempt, in a charming way.

All of it, the terrible intangible strangeness of objects and the thoughts they awakened, struck him the moment he entered the room, and he had recoiled as a thin black wall rose before him, steep and solid, impenetrable, reaching heavenward to the rim of eternity.

He sighed deeply, inhaled as well the reek of vapors now filling the hall with smoke, and felt a quick, strong wave of nausea, suddenly aware of how tired and hungry he was.

He felt his face collapse; his eyes were aching: a gnawing suction deep in the hollows of his eyes, a tormenting, piercing pain he often experienced at the end of a sleepless night. He reinserted the key cautiously in the lock, stumbled into the room, pulled the door closed behind him, and slowly removed the knapsack he carried on his back with a long strap. Then he bent over, felt along the carpet to the left of the door, and slowly slid to the floor. It was wonderful to lie down and stretch out his legs, the knapsack, as so often, under his head.

It must be almost seven. Although he knew her heart beat for him, lovingly and calmly, more lovingly than any other heart ever could, he felt somewhere deep inside that she would not be his, that he would have to relinquish her to something he'd never felt before, something ineffable, stretching from her frayed shoelace to the clouds she sometimes gazed at with thoughts he knew nothing about. He would lose her to the world, that world where it was always so easy to contemplate death, so hard to think of life.

The striped light from the window fell in enlarged form upon the door and wall, a dissolving rectangle, soft and blurred, the white stripes glimmering, the black ones hazy, and he saw that the large black crucifix from the vestibule was now hanging here.

He was oppressed once more by the room's foreignness, a room that wasn't his, by the strange, clean smell of soft soap, clothes, and a hint of cigarette smoke. He rose quickly, picked up his knapsack, and opened the door. As he turned the key in the lock, he wondered for whom the note on the door had been intended. But the thought aroused no hint of jealousy. No, he wasn't jealous of other men. They were all the same, they were all lonely; it was the world he envied so, and the thoughts that filled it.

One of the doors leading into the hall was now standing open, and he could tell by the odor that this was where the fish, onions, and vinegar were being prepared. The vapors filled the room to overflowing and were now seeping into the hall in lukewarm, overpowering waves. He could hear what were apparently raw potatoes being tossed into a pan of sizzling grease; then the bubbling grease gradually subsided to a low, steady crackle as dark gray clouds of vapor billowed from the room, trailing toward the stairwell in soft, slender tendrils. The noise increased, and now and then a door opened. He walked slowly toward the open door and stood for a moment along the opposite wall, watching a short, fat older woman with her left hand stuck in the top of her blouse, slowly turning potatoes in a pan. On an unsanitary-looking table stood a huge porcelain bowl in which gleaming blue fish swam in vinegar, and he could make out the now yellowed sliced onions surrounding them. The entire room was illuminated through a single small pane of glass set in a wooden frame within roughly cemented blocks, which apparently could not be opened. On the kitchen counter—worn, faded, covered with reddish lacquer—stood a bread canister and a scale. He spotted an alarm clock and saw that it was twenty minutes to seven.

He walked back slowly to the stairwell and descended. The white stucco decorations on the ceiling and walls were now defaced islands, scrawled for the most part with all sorts of graffiti.

Descending slowly, step by step, he wondered if he should leave.

Perhaps, he thought, it would be better to go now, before I discover I have no choice; I may spare the menacing angel with the sword the painful duty of driving me out, of watching over my departure with torch and sword. Perhaps I may kneel humbly at the angel's feet, on the threshold, kneel two minutes in his presence, bearing the burden of the last thirty years of my life on my knees.

He paused on a landing and looked through a broken section in the board planks into the back garden. There was the small rusty gate through which he had left back then. It led to a neighboring property, with a well-preserved, well-tended garden; the house, newly roofed and plastered, radiated affluence, security, and serenity. The long, shiny, handsomely painted shutters could close at night or for evening banquets, covering the equally charming, tall and narrow windows. The lawn had been turned and newly seeded. He saw the tiny, deliciously soft shimmer of the first touch of green, the soft down of spring, saw the flower beds with their orderly rows of pansies, and a slender young woman at the side of an equally slender young man, smiling proudly as they strolled slowly along, admiring their garden. The woman was wearing a long, dark brown dress, somewhat darker than the reddish tone of her luxuriantly gleaming hair, with a high-necked yellow sweater, which revealed a narrow strip of her blindingly white throat, like a simple but precious necklace. They looked like clever mechanical dolls, with clever smiles, carefully nuanced, well tempered. Their gestures and steps were so skillfully rehearsed there was no need to note that they were stand-ins in a film that would come to a surprisingly strange end.

He continued slowly to the ground floor and saw that the children were still playing ball at the entrance. It was lovely the way the plump balls flew back and forth so cheerfully in the gray frame of bright light at the door, bouncing softly off the sandstone pilasters, and he heard the bright, eager, unflagging count of the young girls' voices in the contest.

Only now that he was outside did he realize that people must be living in the cellar as well. Rusty brown pipes jutted out of the openings, emitting smoke along with all sorts of cooking odors. Behind the windows, which extended halfway above ground level, he could see a few dismal yellow lights. He heard a radio and voices, and suddenly realized that his hands, seemingly listless within his pockets, were perspiring with fear: He feared the music coming from overbearing mechanical speakers throughout the world, feared the piping, soft, congested voices that undermined the world with their calm, soft security. No place was safe from this so-called music, a steady stream of slime dripping into the ears of humanity from a million speakers. And the smell of onions, fish, vinegar, and fried potatoes permeated the world. He wanted to bury himself deep in the earth and plug his ears, and only now and then, taking a shallow breath, listen to the song of silence, the gentle and lost fragments of paradise.

He wiped his hands on the inner lining of his pockets and walked slowly to the bench where he had been sitting with the old man just a few minutes ago. Having waited years to see her again, the prospect of waiting another hour filled him with a frantic impatience that left him indecisive. He didn't know where to go, the pale wall of her room stood clearly before his eyes, the play of light and shadow from the shutter forming a pattern of silver and black stripes upon it, and over the door the large black crucifix with the white body. He longed to be there on the carpet, the knapsack under his head, looking at the crucifix and waiting, perhaps sleeping as well, but he knew that he would flee from this strange void again, this solid black wall, invisible yet real, thin yet unutterably strong. This wall kept him from entering, throwing open the window, and taking possession of everything, the bed, the view from the window, kept him from gazing out toward the city on the distant horizon, now leveled flat, that he had glimpsed for a moment back then. He had always known the past could never be restored, but actually to experience the fact was frightening. Never, never again . . . Yet he knew she would never forget him. The trace of his eyes on the things in her room could never be effaced, sharper than the bold and regal line of the firmest brush was the trace of his eyes upon her forehead, upon the painting, the carpet, upon the distant horizon, upon every tiny place on her body.

He saw a man working with a shovel and hoe in another garden plot. He went up to him, looked into a tired, unfriendly face, lit his pipe, still half-filled with tobacco, and sat down on the bench, staring at the ground, which was brown, a dark, moist brown, slightly damp, flecked with traces of the white gravel that had once covered the entire semicircular area. The white specks had turned dark; the gradients of the path had been rolled and flattened. Here and there cornstalks, now rotted black, had been trampled into the path, along with rusty nails, burned matches with blackened heads, and in the center, half of a black trouser button.

His thought about the marble-white benches on the clef-shaped paths through the shrubbery, almost certainly overgrown, now struck him as foolish. He had intended to seek out the bench on the left of the grove, to make his way through the undergrowth and touch its cold, damp surface, but now all he could remember was the fear he'd felt as, leaving that very bench, he had emerged from the grove with Maria and approached the terrace, where laughing guests were drinking wine and chatting softly in the mild humidity of a warm autumn evening.

He had paused at the rim of the fountain, looking up at her room on the upper story by the dangling gutter, already feeling the pain of departure. The house stood quiet and calm, wrapped in twilight; between the rows of poplars he had glimpsed the bright dresses of the women, the glowing tips of cigars, heard the voice of a young woman hired to sing. Only a few people lived in the house back then, it was always quiet, always slightly run-down.

At the fountain's rim he had taken his leave. They'll have to have it repaired, he thought, looking at the dangling gutter. Walking past everyone, he led Maria toward her room. Once inside the door of the building she had walked ahead of him, and in the half darkness of the hall he had seen the long folds of her gray dress, her white throat, and as she turned to step into the room, her soft profile.

Later, in Romania, in a White city, he had entered a shop to barter two handkerchiefs and a pair of socks. It was evening, a lively dark bustle of gray uniforms in the narrow lanes, men in long white coattails, and women. All was quiet and gloomy, filled with the voluptuousness of dissolution and decline. They were near the front, and they could hear the impact of the shells, not the soft, thick sound of dough being pounded in the distance, but close by, strident and savage, as if the earth were a piece of flimsy plywood smashed and splintered by hammers. Sometimes they even heard machine-gun fire, rapid and hopeless, like the grinding of worn-out brakes. In one of those streets that at first seem totally empty and turn out to be teeming with life, he stepped into a store, opened a door that led into the darkness, and found himself in a secondhand shop where musty-smelling clothes dangled on hangers from dismal racks, like corpses hanging their heads, their legs amputated. Cheap knickknacks, utensils, Japanese figurines, and watches damned to inactivity stood behind the clothes racks on bluish shelves. He leaned against the low, greasy counter and lit a cigarette.

Suddenly a young Jewish boy emerged silently behind the counter, pale, his face a mixture of boldness, fear, and nameless sadness. He laid his brand-new handkerchiefs on the counter along with the pair of socks. The boy shook his head gently, then was shoved aside by a woman wearing a wrinkled yellow dress. Her profile reminded him of Maria's, as she emerged with him from the garden, walking ahead.

The woman greeted him with a silent nod. He watched as she bent over his things, and her thick hair seemed a dark, dark green. Her hands fingered the linens and he saw that they were small and surprisingly delicate, like the hands of a child. The linens disappeared quietly and briskly under the counter and a banknote lay pale blue against the black wood of the counter. Then she covered the banknote quickly with one hand, lifted her head, and in her face, pale and pretty, with painted lips, he read a weary, indifferent offer.

He took the banknote quickly and banged the door behind him, leaving the clothescorpses swaying slightly on their racks and the Japanese figurines and utensils rattling against one another. He hurried back to the main street, and although it was almost jammed solid with fleeing people, with tanks, some of them damaged, and with carts, and although orders were being shouted to awaken a sense of urgency, he went into a tavern and drank the money up. A crowd of soldiers in the tavern were saying there was still plenty of time, things weren't so bad, the Russians didn't have the strength to advance any farther, and he learned that the front was just two miles off, if it could still be called a front. Then he turned to wine and schnapps, drowning his fear of the secondhand shop with its hanging clothescorpses, the boy, and the profile of the woman who smiled at him with lethargic willingness. Later, because he had a slight leg wound, a medical corps sergeant let him jump on a train for the wounded as it was leaving a station, steadily shelled at regular intervals by the Russians.

As he gazed at the tips of his shoes, sharply outlined against the brown soil mixed with gravel, everything came back to him, how in the dark train rumbling into the night, someone had given him a piece of sausage reeking of garlic, and a dry, musty piece of bread. He had been dying of thirst, and only later, much later, after rocking through an interminable night, at a dark and crowded station platform where people were huddled silently for the night, did they receive a little coffee, in a small tin can.

That's how it always was: He would recall Maria's throat, or her profile, and a myriad memories would tumble after them, as if the first small image were simply the initial link in an infinitely long chain that must glide through him whether he wished it or not. But he forced back these thoughts, stared again at the black tips of his English military shoes, and tried to imagine what lay ahead.

Sometimes he tried to imagine he would find some job to

earn a little money, enough to lie in that room, on the bed. Now he tried to picture what it would be like on the bed, his gaze fixed on the crucifix that would always be in her field of vision. Maria would be standing at the stove, delicate and slightly helpless, and he would ask her please not to fix fish with vinegar and sliced onions, and perhaps the window would be standing open, and the rain would pour through the broken gutter, and the poplars would shield her room from the echo of countless radios.

But suddenly he realized that another pair of shoes had entered his field of vision. They were beautiful, brown, high-quality men's oxfords, cleaned and polished, looking as if they belonged in a display case, yet standing on the edge of the small path, the heels projecting halfway over the furrow. He had always liked his own shoes, black English military-issue shoes from camp, but now they seemed crude, ugly, and shapeless compared to these handsome, polished, high-quality store-window shoes. But the shoes in a store window lacked socks, nor were they topped by soft, light brown, good-looking trousers that almost matched, with a crease that seemed to have a long, sharp knife hidden inside.

He knocked out his pipe, realizing he couldn't have been smoking more than three minutes on what little tobacco he had left, and he thought how long three minutes could be, how it could last years and years. He lifted his head, looked into a face, and knew that he would never lie on the bed, staring at the black crucifix on the green wall, that Maria would never stand at the stove, that he would never let the rain pour through the damaged gutter. He knew it, even though he realized that short of death, there was nothing that must surely come to pass.

The face was calm and broad, the mouth somewhat thin, the eyes slightly narrow, but the forehead was high and noble; his hair, however, was curly, combed with unnecessary care; he had never liked men with wavy hair. . . .

In the matching hands below, the man carried a brown attaché case, and pressed against the attaché case with the thumb, a soft, light gray hat, with an immaculate sweatband.

The man said to him: "Oh, I see, you're the one over her bed." And he said the same thing he'd said to the pretty woman: "Probably so."

Then he took his hand from his pocket, still clutching the note, which he undid carefully, and held it out, saying: "This must be for you. . . ."

"Oh, yes," said the other, "it's for me. So she'll be back at eight." And he looked at his wristwatch and said: "Over an hour yet."

They looked at each other, the man chewing on his lower lip, and he, on the bench, knew now that she belonged to this man, to him alone, and that nothing and no one in the world could take her from him, just as surely as he knew that he would never lie upon that bed.

Now they looked past each other, and then he looked at the ground again and saw that the man's shoes were tapping restlessly. He kept tapping his toes, and between the tips of the shoes, separated by the regulation distance, the man sitting on the bench saw half of a black trouser button, trampled into the ground.

"Perhaps," the voice now said above him, "we should spend the hour in conversation."

I stood up and followed him, and as I stood, in that tenth of a second, that fractional fraction of the tiniest space of time, I knew that she was lost to me, finally and irrevocably. As long as the garden paths were too narrow to walk side by side he remained in front of me, then he paused for a moment as we reached the broader paths, let me draw up alongside him, and we walked back in silence on the long, straight path that led through the grove toward the entrance, to that rusted gate no one opened anymore. Then we turned left toward one of the gaps in the wall, and I saw a car parked under the thick green roof of the trees, a black, high-quality, solid, and expensive piece of workmanship, reliable, clean, rugged, and sturdy. We slowed down as we approached one of the largest gaps; now we stopped and looked at each other. I saw he was trembling, his lips quivered, the solid, large, well-formed face seemed to come unhinged, and he said to me: "We were married yesterday, no one knows." I simply nodded, looked at the ground, and then at him again.

His eyes spoke a huge truth of which he could not be aware—together with his pain, his poverty, his trembling, all his unknown, repressed pain—the truth that there are things that can't be bought or won, that can only come as a gift, and one of these is love.

I nodded again and walked away. I climbed carefully over the wall, crossed the avenue, and made my way along a rough, treeless road toward the city, where I could catch a train. Behind me the sun stood low on the horizon, casting my shadow so far forward that I could scarcely see the large round dot of my head. Only when I came to some obstacle, a fence, a shed, or a partially collapsed wall, would the shadow of my head pause before me, growing larger and larger, until it flowed beyond the object it had struck, flying from me again, far, far away, so far beyond my flat field of vision that I could no longer see it, and I knew that I would never, never reach it again.

a note on the text

THE STORIES PRINTED HERE are based on the original German typescripts from Heinrich Böll's literary estate, as preserved by the heirs and placed in the Heinrich Böll Archive of the city of Cologne, Germany.

The original typescripts are in various stages of completion. The German editors corrected obvious typographical errors, restored missing words, and made other small emendations. They made no attempt to correct inconsistencies or factual errors of the sort often present in working typescripts. For example, they retained the alternation in narrative perspective in "Paradise Lost," although they believe Böll would have unified it eventually, and they left untouched several inconsistent references to the length of time until the woman is to return (the time has been rendered consistent in the English version). The German editors introduced what they consider consistent punctuation in order to make the text more readable, and in the belief that Böll's own practice of revising these and other texts shows he would surely have done this.

The stories have been arranged in roughly chronological order for the American edition. Where typescripts were undated, the German editors turned to the author's notebooks and correspondence, and to the type of paper used, in order to determine their approximate dates of composition.

Upon this basis, the following dates were established:

"The Fugitive": The fair copy is dated November 2–3, 1946, and was sent on May 12, 1947, to the *Frankfurter Hefte.*

"Youth on Fire": A note accompanying the typescript gives the dates December 18, 1936, and March 3 and 7, 1937.

"Trapped in Paris": Dated December 25, 1946. A now-missing fair copy of the text was sent to the periodical *Karussell* in Kassel on May 31, 1947, and to *Die Fähre* in Munich on June 27, 1947.

"The Mad Dog": The typescript is dated February 10–11, 1947. It was sent to the periodical *Das Goldene Tor* in Baden-Baden on May 31, 1947.

"The Rendezvous": First draft dated August 11, 1948; a second, revised version, published here, is undated. The story was first submitted to the Stuttgart radio station on August 13, 1948, and offered to various newspapers and periodicals through 1952.

"The Tribe of Esau": Undated typescript; the paper used would point to a date of composition around 1948/49.

"The Tale of Berkovo Bridge": Undated, presumably written toward the end of 1948. Böll suggested it for the collection *Wanderer, kommst du nach Spa . . . (Traveler, If You Come to Spa . . .)* but in the end it was not included there. Böll finally worked it into the eighth chapter of his novel *Wo warst du, Adam? (And Where Were You, Adam?)* in 1951. This version was subsequently transformed into a radio play in 1952, under the title "Die Brücke von Berczaba" (Berczaba Bridge).

"The Dead No Longer Obey": The untitled typescript is dated January 5, 1949. The present title is indicated on an early draft, and was repeated by Böll in a list of titles dated January 8, 1949. The text is a reworking of a passage from the draft of a play by Böll entitled "Wie das Gesetz es befahl" *(As the Law Demanded),* which also dates from January 1949.

"America": Undated; based on the type of paper used, probably around 1950.

"Paradise Lost": Novel fragment. The manuscript broke off after the second chapter. The text printed here consists of the first chapter. Böll noted May 1, 2, and 4 as the date of the initial chapter in his notebook of 1949. Some passages were incorporated in revised form in *Der Engel schwieg (The Silent Angel),* which Böll began in that same year. Two shorter stories from "Paradise Lost" were published earlier under the titles "Die Liebesnacht" ("Night of Love") and "Die Dachrinne" ("The Gutter").

ABOUT THE AUTHOR

Heinrich Böll was the first German to win the Nobel Prize for literature (in 1972) since Thomas Mann in 1929. Born in Cologne in 1917, Böll was raised in a liberal Catholic, pacifist family. Drafted into the Wehrmacht, he served on the Russian and French fronts and was wounded four times before he found himself in an American prisoner-of-war camp.

After the war, Böll enrolled at the University of Cologne, but dropped out to write about his shattering experiences as a soldier. A master storyteller, he wrote a host of novels and short stories. He was President of the International P.E.N. and an eloquent defender of the intellectual freedom of writers throughout the world.

Heinrich Böll died in Cologne on July 16, 1985.

ABOUT THE TRANSLATOR

Breon Mitchell received the D. Phil. in Modern Languages from Oxford University and is currently Director of the Wells Scholars Program at Indiana University. He has received a number of national awards, including the American Translators Association German Literary Prize in 1987, the 1992 ALTA Translation Prize, and the Theodore Christian Hoepfner Award in 1995.